Dear Reader,

There has never been a magical kingdom quite like Oz. Populated by good witches and wicked witches, wretched Nomes and enchanting princesses, chattering hens and cowardly lions—a whole host of marvelous creatures great and small and wise and wonderful—Oz is one of the most beloved fantasy worlds ever created.

The enormous explosion of all types of fantasy that we are seeing in today's market makes us feel that now is the time for a brilliantly successful Oz revival.

When we mention Oz to people who haven't grown up with the books, they nod, mention Judy Garland and think they know all there is to know about Oz. How wrong they are! They have no idea how rich the series is, how many wonderful characters and creatures there are. We have every expectation of making Oz as familiar to millions of fantasy readers as is Tolkien's Middle-earth and Lewis's Narnia.

Del Rey Books is now publishing the original fourteen Baum Oz books.

Come, join us in Oz.

Magically,
Judy-Lynn & Lester del Rey
Del Rey Books

Oz IS...

"Oz—where the young stay young and the old grow young forever—these books are for readers of all ages."
        —Ray Bradbury

"Who says the Land of Oz is only for the young? Age has nothing to do with it. Oz belongs to the young at heart and always will. All that is needed is an adventuresome spirit and a genuine affection for classic fantasy."
        —Terry Brooks
          Author of *The Sword of Shannara*

"I was raised with the Oz books, and their enchantment, humor and excitement remain with me. They are still a joy and a treasure. I welcome this Oz revival."
        —Stephen R. Donaldson
          Author of *The Chronicles of Thomas Covenant*

"The land of Oz has managed to fascinate each new generation . . . the Oz books continue to exert their spell . . . and those who read [them] are often made what they were not—imaginative, tolerant, alert to wonders, life."
        —Gore Vidal
          The New York Review of Books

The Wonderful Oz Books by L. Frank Baum
Now Published by Del Rey Books

*Coming Soon from Del Rey Books

THE
LOST PRINCESS
OF OZ

BY

L. FRANK BAUM

AUTHOR OF

The Road to Oz, Dorothy and the Wizard in Oz, The
Emerald City of Oz, The Land of Oz, Ozma of Oz,
The Patchwork Girl of Oz, Tik-Tok of
Oz, The Scarecrow of Oz,
Rinkitink in Oz

ILLUSTRATED BY

JOHN R. NEILL

A Del Rey Book

BALLANTINE BOOKS · NEW YORK

A Del Rey Book
Published by Ballantine Books

"The Marvelous Land of Oz" Map copyright © 1979 by James E. Haff and Dick Martin. Reproduced by permission of The International Wizard of Oz Club, Inc.

Published in the United States by Ballantine Books, a division of Random House, Inc., New York, and simultaneously in Canada by Random House of Canada, Limited, Toronto, Canada.

Library of Congress Catalog Card Number: 77-75861

ISBN 0-345-28233-7

This edition published by arrangement with Contemporary Books, Inc.

Maunfactured in the United States of America

First Ballantine Books Edition: December 1980

Cover art by Michael Herring

This Book is Dedicated
To My Granddaughter
OZMA BAUM

To My Readers

Some of my youthful readers are developing wonderful imaginations. This pleases me. Imagination has brought mankind through the Dark Ages to its present state of civilization. Imagination led Columbus to discover America. Imagination led Franklin to discover electricity. Imagination has given us the steam engine, the telephone, the talking-machine and the automobile, for these things had to be dreamed of before they became realities. So I believe that dreams—day dreams, you know, with your eyes wide open and your brain-machinery whizzing—are likely to lead to the betterment of the world. The imaginative child will become the imaginative man or woman most apt to create, to invent, and therefore to foster civilization. A prominent educator tells me that fairy tales are of untold value in developing imagination in the young. I believe it.

Among the letters I receive from children are many containing suggestions of "what to write about in the next Oz Book." Some of the ideas advanced are mighty interesting, while others are too extravagant to be seriously considered—even in a fairy tale. Yet I like them all, and I must admit that the main idea in "The Lost Princess of Oz" was sug-

To My Readers

gested to me by a sweet little girl of eleven who called to see me and to talk about the Land of Oz. Said she: "I s'pose if Ozma ever got lost, or stolen, ev'rybody in Oz would be dreadful sorry."

That was all, but quite enough foundation to build this present story on. If you happen to like the story, give credit to my little friend's clever hint.

L. Frank Baum
Royal Historian of Oz

List of Chapters

THE LOST

PRINCESS

OF

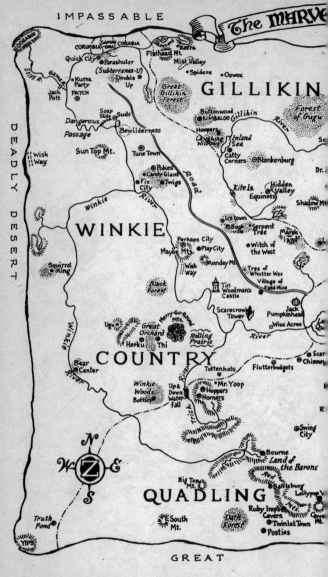

IMPASSABLE

The MARVE

OGABOO · CORUMBIA · SARAH-DRA · CORABIA
Quick City · Parashuter · Flathead · Rada
Stiff R. · (Subterranea-U) · Mist Valley
Gama · Kuma Party · Double Up · Spiders · Ozwoz
Jack Pott · PATCH
Soap Slide · Suds · Buttonwood · Gillikin · Forest of Gugu
Dangerous Passage · Bewilderness · KIMBALOO
GILLIKIN
Hoopers · Laughing Willows · Gillikin River
Sun Top Mt. · Tune Town · Inland Sea
Catty Corners · Blankenburg
Pokes · Candy Giant · Twigs · Kite Is. · Hidden Valley
Fix City · Equinots · Shadow Mt.
Ice town · Boo ville · Serpent Tree · Marsh Land
Winkie River
WINKIE · Perhaps City · Maybe Mts. · Play City · Witch of the West
Wish Way · Monday Mt. · Tree of Whutter Wee · Village of Field Mice
Squirrel King · Black Forest · Tin Woodman's Castle
Scarecrow's Tower · Jack Pumpkinhead
Winkie River · Ugu · Great Orchard · Thi · Merry-Go-Round Mts. · Wise Acres
Herku · Rolling Prairie
COUNTRY · River · Scar Chimney
Bear Center · Tottenhots · Flutterbudgets
Winkie Woods Bottles · Up & Down Water fall · Mr. Yoop · Hoppers · Horners
Trick River · Swing City
Bourne · Land of the Barons
N W Z E S · Big Top Mt. · Red · Battlefurg · Lollypop
QUADLING · Ness · Carro Mt.
Truth Pond · South Mt. · Dark Forest · Ruby Imp's Cavern · Twinlet Town
YIPS · Posties

GREAT

© 1979 by James E. Haff and Dick Martin.
Reproduced by permission of The International Wizard of
Oz Club, Inc.

A Terrible Loss

CHAPTER 1

THERE could be no doubt of the fact: Princess Ozma, the lovely girl ruler of the Fairyland of Oz, was lost. She had completely disappeared. Not one of her subjects— not even her closest friends—knew what had become of her.

It was Dorothy who first discovered it. Dorothy was a little Kansas girl who had come to the Land of Oz to live and had been given a delightful suite of rooms in Ozma's royal palace, just because Ozma loved Dorothy and wanted her to live as near her as possible, so the two girls might be much together.

Dorothy was not the only girl from the outside world who had been welcomed to Oz and lived in the royal palace. There was another named Betsy Bobbin, whose adventures had led her to seek refuge with Ozma, and still another named Trot, who had been invited, together with her faithful companion, Cap'n Bill, to make her home in this wonderful fairyland. The three girls all had rooms in the palace and were great chums; but Dorothy was the dearest friend of their gracious Ruler and only she at any hour dared to seek Ozma in her royal apartments. For Dorothy had lived in Oz much longer than the other girls and had been made a Princess of the realm.

Betsy was a year older than Dorothy and Trot was a year younger, yet the three were near enough of an age to become great playmates and to have nice times together. It was while the three were talking together one morning in Dorothy's room that Betsy proposed they make a journey into the Munchkin Country, which was one of the four great countries of the Land of Oz ruled by Ozma.

"I've never been there yet," said Betsy Bobbin, "but the Scarecrow once told me it is the prettiest country in all Oz."

"I'd like to go, too," added Trot.

"All right," said Dorothy, "I'll go and ask Ozma. Perhaps she will let us take the Saw-horse and the Red Wagon, which would be much nicer for us than having to walk all the

way. This Land of Oz is a pretty big place, when you get to all the edges of it."

So she jumped up and went along the halls of the splendid palace until she came to the royal suite, which filled all the front of the second floor. In a little waiting room sat Ozma's maid, Jellia Jamb, who was busily sewing.

"Is Ozma up yet?" inquired Dorothy.

"I don't know, my dear," replied Jellia. "I haven't heard a word from her this morning. She hasn't even called for her bath or her breakfast, and it is far past her usual time for them."

"That's strange!" exclaimed the little girl.

"Yes," agreed the maid; "but of course no harm could have happened to her. No one can die or be killed in the Land of Oz and Ozma is herself a powerful fairy, and she has no enemies, so far as we know. Therefore I am not at all worried about her, though I must admit her silence is unusual."

"Perhaps," said Dorothy, thoughtfully, "she has overslept. Or she may be reading, or working out some new sort of magic to do good to her people."

"Any of these things may be true," replied Jellia Jamb, "so I haven't dared disturb our royal mistress. You, however, are a privileged character, Princess, and I am sure that Ozma wouldn't mind at all if you went in to see her."

"Of course not," said Dorothy, and opening

the door of the outer chamber she went in. All was still here. She walked into another room, which was Ozma's boudoir, and then, pushing back a heavy drapery richly broidered with threads of pure gold, the girl entered the sleeping-room of the fairy Ruler of Oz. The bed of ivory and gold was vacant; the room was vacant; not a trace of Ozma was to be found.

Very much surprised, yet still with no fear that anything had happened to her friend, Dorothy returned through the boudoir to the other rooms of the suite. She went into the music room, the library, the laboratory, the bath, the wardrobe and even into the great throne room, which adjoined the royal suite, but in none of these places could she find Ozma.

So she returned to the anteroom where she had left the maid, Jellia Jamb, and said:

"She isn't in her rooms now, so she must have gone out."

"I don't understand how she could do that without my seeing her," replied Jellia, "unless she made herself invisible."

"She isn't there, anyhow," declared Dorothy.

"Then let us go find her," suggested the maid, who appeared to be a little uneasy.

So they went into the corridors and there Dorothy almost stumbled over a queer girl who was dancing lightly along the passage.

"Stop a minute, Scraps!" she called. "Have

you seen Ozma this morning?"

"Not I!" replied the queer girl, dancing nearer. "I lost both my eyes in a tussle with the Woozy, last night, for the creature scraped 'em both off my face with his square paws. So I put the eyes in my pocket and this morning Button-Bright led me to Aunt Em, who sewed 'em on again. So I've seen nothing at all to-day, except during the last five minutes. So of course I haven't seen Ozma."

"Very well, Scraps," said Dorothy, looking curiously at the eyes, which were merely two round black buttons sewed upon the girl's face.

There were other things about Scraps that would have seemed curious to one seeing her for the first time. She was commonly called "The Patchwork Girl," because her body and limbs were made from a gay-colored patchwork quilt which had been cut into shape and stuffed with cotton. Her head was a round ball stuffed in the same manner and fastened to her shoulders. For hair she had a mass of brown yarn and to make a nose for her a part of the cloth had been pulled out into the shape of a knob and tied with a string to hold it in place. Her mouth had been carefully made by cutting a slit in the proper place and lining it with red silk, adding two rows of pearls for teeth and a bit of red flannel for a tongue.

In spite of this queer make-up, the Patch-

work Girl was magically alive and had proved herself not the least jolly and agreeable of the many quaint characters who inhabit the astonishing Fairyland of Oz. Indeed, Scraps was a general favorite, although she was rather flighty and erratic and did and said many things that surprised her friends. She was seldom still, but loved to dance, to turn handsprings and somersaults, to climb trees and to indulge in many other active sports.

"I'm going to search for Ozma," remarked Dorothy, "for she isn't in her rooms and I want to ask her a question."

"I'll go with you," said Scraps, "for my eyes are brighter than yours and they can see farther."

"I'm not sure of that," remarked Dorothy. "But come along, if you like."

Together they searched all through the great palace and even to the farthest limits of the palace grounds, which were quite extensive, but nowhere could they find a trace of Ozma. When Dorothy returned to where Betsy and Trot awaited her, the little girl's face was rather solemn and troubled, for never before had Ozma gone away without telling her friends where she was going, or without an escort that befitted her royal state.

She was gone, however, and none had seen her go. Dorothy had met and questioned the Scarecrow, Tik-Tok, the Shaggy Man, Button-

Bright, Cap'n Bill, and even the wise and powerful Wizard of Oz, but not one of them had seen Ozma since she parted with her friends the evening before and had gone to her own rooms.

"She didn't say anything las' night about going anywhere," observed little Trot.

"No, and that's the strange part of it," replied Dorothy. "Usually Ozma lets us know of everything she does."

"Why not look in the Magic Picture?" suggested Betsy Bobbin. "That will tell us where she is, in just one second."

"Of course!" cried Dorothy. "Why didn't I think of that before?" and at once the three girls hurried away to Ozma's boudoir, where the Magic Picture always hung.

This wonderful Magic Picture was one of the royal Ozma's greatest treasures. There was a large gold frame, in the center of which was a bluish-gray canvas on which various scenes constantly appeared and disappeared. If one who stood before it wished to see what any person—anywhere in the world—was doing, it was only necessary to make the wish and the scene in the Magic Picture would shift to the scene where that person was and show exactly what he or she was then engaged in doing. So the girls knew it would be easy for them to wish to see Ozma,

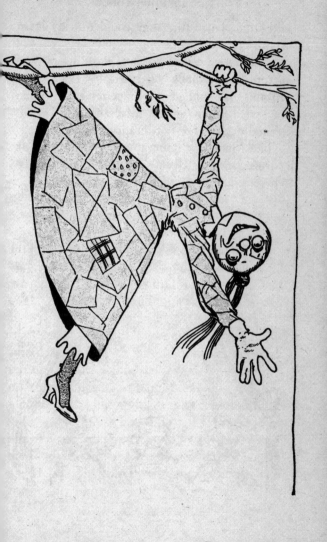

and from the picture they could quickly learn where she was.

Dorothy advanced to the place where the picture was usually protected by thick satin curtains, and pulled the draperies aside. Then she stared in amazement, while her two friends uttered exclamations of disappointment.

The Magic Picture was gone. Only a blank space on the wall behind the curtains showed where it had formerly hung.

The Troubles of Glinda the Good

CHAPTER 2

THAT same morning there was great excitement in the castle of the powerful Sorceress of Oz, Glinda the Good. This castle, situated in the Quadling Country, far south of the Emerald City where Ozma ruled, was a splendid structure of exquisite marbles and silver grilles. Here the Sorceress lived, surrounded by a bevy of the most beautiful maidens of Oz, gathered from all the four countries of that fairy-land as well as from the magnificent Emerald City itself, which stood in the place where the four countries cornered.

It was considered a great honor to be allowed to serve the good Sorceress, whose arts of magic were used only to benefit the Oz people. Glinda was Ozma's most valued servant, for her knowledge of sorcery was wonderful and she could accomplish almost anything that her mistress, the lovely girl Ruler of Oz, wished her to.

Of all the magical things which surrounded Glinda in her castle there was none more marvelous than her Great Book of Records. On the pages of this Record Book were constantly being inscribed—day by day and hour by hour—all the important events that happened anywhere in the known world, and they were inscribed in the book at exactly the moment the events happened. Every adventure in the Land of Oz and in the big outside world, and even in places that you and I have never heard of, were recorded accurately in the Great Book, which never made a mistake and stated only the exact truth. For that reason nothing could be concealed from Glinda the Good, who had only to look at the pages of the Great Book of Records to know everything that had taken place. That was one reason she was such a great Sorceress, for the records made her wiser than any other living person.

This wonderful book was placed upon a big gold table that stood in the middle of Glinda's drawing-room. The legs of the table, which were incrusted with precious gems, were firmly fastened to the tiled floor and the book itself was chained to the table and locked with six stout golden padlocks, the keys to which Glinda carried on a chain that was secured around her own neck.

The pages of the Great Book were larger in size than those of an American newspaper and although they were exceedingly thin there were so many of them that they made an enormous, bulky volume. With its gold cover and gold clasps the book was so heavy that three men could scarcely have lifted it. Yet this morning, when Glinda entered her drawing-room after breakfast, with all her maidens trailing after her, the good Sorceress was amazed to discover that her Great Book of Records had mysteriously disappeared.

Advancing to the table, she found the chains had been cut with some sharp instrument, and this must have been done while all in the castle slept. Glinda was shocked and grieved. Who could have done this wicked, bold thing? And who could wish to deprive her of her Great Book of Records?

The Sorceress was thoughtful for a time, considering the consequences of her loss. Then she went to her Room of Magic to prepare a charm that would tell her who had stolen the Record Book. But, when she unlocked her cupboards and threw open the doors, all of her magical instruments and rare chemical compounds had been removed from the shelves.

The Sorceress was now both angry and alarmed. She sat down in a chair and tried to think how this extraordinary robbery could have taken place. It was evident that the thief was some person of very great power, or the theft could never have been accomplished without her knowledge. But who, in all the Land of Oz, was powerful and skillful enough to do this awful thing? And who, having the power, could also have an object in defying the wisest and most talented Sorceress the world has ever known?

Glinda thought over the perplexing matter for a full hour, at the end of which time she was still puzzled how to explain it. But although her instruments and chemicals were gone her *knowledge* of magic had not been stolen, by any means, since no thief, however skillful, can rob one of knowledge, and that is why knowledge is the best and safest treasure to acquire. Glinda believed that when she had time to gather more magical herbs and elixirs and to manufacture more magical instruments she would be able to discover who the robber was, and what had become of her precious Book of Records.

"Whoever has done this," she said to her maidens, "is a very foolish person, for in time he is sure to be found out and will then be severely punished."

She now made a list of the things she needed

and dispatched messengers to every part of Oz with instructions to obtain them and bring them to her as soon as possible. And one of her messengers met the little Wizard of Oz, who was mounted on the back of the famous live Sawhorse and was clinging to its neck with both his arms; for the Sawhorse was speeding to Glinda's castle with the velocity of the wind, bearing the news that Royal Ozma, Ruler of all the great Land of Oz, had suddenly disappeared and no one in the Emerald City knew what had become of her.

"Also," said the Wizard, as he stood before the astonished Sorceress, "Ozma's Magic Picture is gone, so we cannot consult it to discover where she is. So I came to you for assistance as soon as we realized our loss. Let us look in the Great Book of Records."

"Alas," returned the Sorceress sorrowfully, "we cannot do that, for the Great Book of Records has also disappeared!"

Robbery of Cayke the Cookie Cook

CHAPTER 3

ONE more important theft was reported in the Land of Oz that eventful morning, but it took place so far from either the Emerald City or the castle of Glinda the Good that none of those persons we have mentioned learned of the robbery until long afterward.

In the far southwestern corner of the Winkie Country is a broad tableland that can be reached only by climbing a steep hill, whichever side one approaches it. On the hillside surrounding this tableland are no paths at all, but there are quantities of bramble-bushes with sharp prickers on them, which prevent any of the Oz people who live down below from climbing up to see what is on top. But on top live the Yips, and although the space they occupy is not great in extent the wee country is all their own. The Yips had never—up to the time this story begins—left their broad tableland to go down into the Land of Oz, nor had the Oz people ever climbed up to the country of the Yips.

Living all alone as they did, the Yips had queer ways and notions of their own and did not resemble any other people of the Land of Oz. Their houses were scattered all over the flat surface; not like a city, grouped together, but set wherever their owners' fancy dictated, with fields here, trees there, and odd little paths connecting the houses one with another.

It was here, on the morning when Ozma so strangely disappeared from the Emerald City, that Cayke the Cookie Cook discovered that her diamond-studded gold dishpan had been stolen, and she raised such a hue-and-cry over her loss and wailed and shrieked so loudly that many of the Yips gathered around her house to inquire what was the matter.

It was a serious thing, in any part of the Land of Oz, to accuse one of stealing, so when the Yips heard Cayke the Cookie Cook declare that her jeweled dishpan had been stolen they were both humiliated and disturbed and forced Cayke to go with them to the Frogman to see what could be done about it.

I do not suppose you have ever before heard

of the Frogman, for like all other dwellers on that tableland he had never been away from it, nor had anyone come up there to see him. The Frogman was, in truth, descended from the common frogs of Oz, and when he was first born he lived in a pool in the Winkie Country and was much like any other frog. Being of an adventurous nature, however, he soon hopped out of his pool and began to travel, when a big bird came along and seized him in its beak and started to fly away with him to its nest. When high in the air the frog wriggled so frantically that he got loose and fell down—down—down into a small hidden pool on the tableland of the Yips. Now this pool, it seems, was unknown to the Yips because it was surrounded by thick bushes and was not near to any dwelling, and it proved to be an enchanted pool, for the frog grew very fast and very big, feeding on the magic skosh which is found nowhere else on earth except in that one pool. And the skosh not only made the frog very big, so that when he stood on his hind legs he was tall as any Yip in the country, but it made him unusually intelligent, so that he soon knew more than the Yips did and was able to reason and to argue very well indeed.

No one could expect a frog with these talents to remain in a hidden pool, so he finally got out of it and mingled with the people of the table-

land, who were amazed at his appearance and greatly impressed by his learning. They had never seen a frog before and the frog had never seen a Yip before, but as there were plenty of Yips and only one frog, the frog became the most important. He did not hop any more, but stood upright on his hind legs and dressed himself in fine clothes and sat in chairs and did all the things that people do; so he soon came to be called the Frogman, and that is the only name he has ever had.

After some years had passed the people came to regard the Frogman as their adviser in all matters that puzzled them. They brought all their difficulties to him and when he did not know anything he pretended to know it, which seemed to answer just as well. Indeed, the Yips thought the Frogman was much wiser than he really was, and he allowed them to think so, being very proud of his position of authority.

There was another pool on the tableland, which was not enchanted but contained good clear water and was located close to the dwellings. Here the people built the Frogman a house of his own, close to the edge of the pool, so that he could take a bath or a swim whenever he wished. He usually swam in the pool in the early morning, before anyone else was up, and during the day he dressed himself in his beautiful clothes and sat in his house and received the visits of all the Yips who came to him to ask his advice.

The Frogman's usual costume consisted of knee-breeches made of yellow satin plush, with trimmings of gold braid and jeweled knee-buckles; a white satin vest with silver buttons in which were set solitaire rubies; a swallow-tailed coat of bright yellow; green stockings and red leather shoes turned up at the toes and having diamond buckles. He wore, when he walked out, a purple silk hat and carried a gold-headed cane. Over his eyes he wore great spectacles with gold rims, not because his eyes were bad but because the spectacles made him look wise, and so distinguished and gorgeous was his appearance that all the Yips were very proud of him.

There was no King or Queen in the Yip Country, so the simple inhabitants naturally came to look upon the Frogman as their leader as well as their counselor in all times of emergency. In his heart the big frog knew he was no wiser than the Yips, but for a frog to know as much as a person was quite remarkable, and the Frogman was shrewd enough to make the people believe he was far more wise than he really was. They never suspected he was a humbug, but listened to his words with great respect and did just what he advised them to do.

Now, when Cayke the Cookie Cook raised

such an outcry over the theft of her diamond-studded dishpan, the first thought of the people was to take her to the Frogman and inform him of the loss, thinking that of course he could tell her where to find it.

He listened to the story with his big eyes wide open behind his spectacles, and said in his deep, croaking voice:

"If the dishpan is stolen, somebody must have taken it."

"But who?" asked Cayke, anxiously. "Who is the thief?"

"The one who took the dishpan, of course," replied the Frogman, and hearing this all the Yips nodded their heads gravely and said to one another:

"It is absolutely true!"

"But I want my dishpan!" cried Cayke.

"No one can blame you for that wish," remarked the Frogman.

"Then tell me where I may find it," she urged.

The look the Frogman gave her was a very wise look and he rose from his chair and strutted up and down the room with his hands under his coat-tails, in a very pompous and imposing manner. This was the first time so difficult a matter had been brought to him and he wanted time to think. It would never do to let them suspect his ignorance and so he thought very, very hard how best to answer the woman without betraying himself.

"I beg to inform you," said he, "that nothing in the Yip Country has ever been stolen before."

"We know that, already," answered Cayke the Cookie Cook, impatiently.

"Therefore," continued the Frogman, "this theft becomes a very important matter."

"Well, where is my dishpan?" demanded the woman.

"It is lost; but it must be found. Unfortunately, we have no policemen or detectives to unravel the mystery, so we must employ other means to regain the lost article. Cayke must first write a Proclamation and tack it to the door of her house, and the Proclamation must read that whoever stole the jeweled dishpan must return it at once."

"But suppose no one returns it," suggested Cayke.

"Then," said the Frogman, "that very fact will be proof that no one has stolen it."

Cayke was not satisfied, but the other Yips seemed to approve the plan highly. They all advised her to do as the Frogman had told her to, so she posted the sign on her door and waited patiently for someone to return the dishpan— which no one ever did.

Again she went, accompanied by a group of her neighbors, to the Frogman, who by this time had given the matter considerable thought. Said he to Cayke:

"I am now convinced that no Yip has taken your dishpan, and, since it is gone from the Yip Country, I suspect that some stranger came from the world down below us, in the darkness of night when all of us were asleep, and took away your treasure. There can be no other explanation of its disappearance. So, if you wish to recover that golden, diamond-studded dishpan, you must go into the lower world after it."

This was indeed a startling proposition. Cayke and her friends went to the edge of the flat tableland and looked down the steep hillside to the plains below. It was so far to the bottom of the hill that nothing there could be seen very distinctly and it seemed to the Yips very venturesome, if not dangerous, to go so far from home into an unknown land.

However, Cayke wanted her dishpan very badly, so she turned to her friends and asked:

"Who will go with me?"

No one answered this question, but after a period of silence one of the Yips said:

"We know what is here, on the top of this flat hill, and it seems to us a very pleasant place; but what is down below we do not know. The chances are it is not so pleasant, so we had best stay where we are."

"It may be a far better country than this is,"

suggested the Cookie Cook.

"Maybe, maybe," responded another Yip, "but why take chances? Contentment with one's lot is true wisdom. Perhaps, in some other country, there are better cookies than you cook; but as we have always eaten your cookies, and liked them—except when they are burned on the bottom—we do not long for any better ones."

Cayke might have agreed to this argument had she not been so anxious to find her precious dishpan, but now she exclaimed impatiently:

"You are cowards—all of you! If none of you are willing to explore with me the great world beyond this small hill, I will surely go alone."

"That is a wise resolve," declared the Yips, much relieved. "It is your dispan that is lost, not ours; and, if you are willing to risk your life and liberty to regain it, no one can deny you the privilege."

While they were thus conversing the Frogman joined them and looked down at the plain with his big eyes and seemed unusually thoughtful. In fact, the Frogman was thinking that he'd like to see more of the world. Here in the Yip Country he had become the most important creature of them all and his importance was getting to be a little tame. It would be nice to have other people defer to him and ask his advice and there seemed no reason, so far as he could see, why his fame should not spread throughout all Oz.

He knew nothing of the rest of the world, but it was reasonable to believe that there were more people beyond the mountain where he now lived than there were Yips, and if he went among them he could surprise them with his display of wisdom and make them bow down to him as the Yips did. In other words, the Frogman was ambitious to become still greater than he was, which was impossible if he always remained upon this mountain. He wanted others to see his gorgeous clothes and listen to his solemn sayings, and here was an excuse for him to get away from the Yip Country. So he said to Cayke the Cookie Cook:

"I will go with you, my good woman," which greatly pleased Cayke because she felt the Frogman could be of much assistance to her in her search.

But now, since the mighty Frogman had decided to undertake the journey, several of the Yips who were young and daring at once made up their minds to go along; so the next morning after breakfast the Frogman and Cayke the Cookie Cook and nine of the Yips started to slide down the side of the mountain. The bramble bushes and cactus plants were very prickly and uncomfortable to the touch, so the Frogman commanded the Yips to go first and break a path, so that when he followed them he would not tear his splendid clothes. Cayke, too, was wearing her best dress, and was likewise afraid of the thorns and prickers, so she kept behind the Frogman.

They made rather slow progress and night overtook them before they were halfway down the mountain side, so they found a cave in which they sought shelter until morning. Cayke had brought along a basket full of her famous cookies, so they all had plenty to eat.

On the second day the Yips began to wish they had not embarked on this adventure. They grumbled a good deal at having to cut away the thorns to make the path for the Frogman and the Cookie Cook, for their own clothing suffered many tears, while Cayke and the Frogman traveled safely and in comfort.

"If it is true that anyone came to our country to steal your diamond dishpan," said one of the Yips to Cayke, "it must have been a bird, for no person in the form of a man, woman or child could have climbed through these bushes and back again."

"And, allowing he could have done so," said another Yip, "the diamond-studded gold dishpan would not have repair him for his troubles and his tribulations."

"For my part," remarked a third Yip, "I would rather go back home and dig and polish some more diamonds, and mine some more gold, and make you another dishpan, than be scratched from head to heel by these dreadful bushes. Even now, if my mother saw me, she would not know I am her son."

Cayke paid no heed to these mutterings, nor did the Frogman. Although their journey was slow it was being made easy for them by the Yips, so they had nothing to complain of and no desire to turn back.

Quite near to the bottom of the great hill they came upon a deep gulf, the sides of which were as smooth as glass. The gulf extended a long distance—as far as they could see, in either direction—and although it was not very wide it was far too wide for the Yips to leap across it. And, should they fall into it, it was likely they might never get out again.

"Here our journey ends," said the Yips. "We must go back again."

Cayke the Cookie Cook began to weep.

"I shall never find my pretty dishpan again—and my heart will be broken!" she sobbed.

The Frogman went to the edge of the gulf and with his eye carefully measured the distance to the other side.

"Being a frog," said he, "I can leap, as all frogs do; and, being so big and strong, I am sure I can leap across this gulf with ease. But the rest of you, not being frogs, must return the way you came."

"We will do that with pleasure," cried the Yips and at once they turned and began to climb up the steep mountain, feeling they had had quite enough of this unsatisfactory adventure. Cayke the Cookie Cook did not go with them, however. She sat on a rock and wept and wailed and was very miserable.

"Well," said the Frogman to her, "I will now bid you good-bye. If I find your diamond decorated gold dishpan I will promise to see that it is safely returned to you."

"But I prefer to find it myself!" she said. "See here, Frogman, why can't you carry me across the gulf when you leap it? You are big and strong, while I am small and thin."

The Frogman gravely thought over this suggestion. It was a fact that Cayke the Cookie Cook was not a heavy person. Perhaps he could leap the gulf with her on his back.

"If you are willing to risk a fall," said he, "I will make the attempt."

At once she sprang up and grabbed him around his neck with both her arms. That is, she grabbed him where his neck ought to be, for the Frogman had no neck at all. Then he squatted down, as frogs do when they leap, and with his powerful rear legs he made a tremendous jump.

Over the gulf he sailed, with the Cookie Cook on his back, and he had leaped so hard—to make sure of not falling in—that he sailed over a lot of bramble-bushes that grew on the other side and landed in a clear space which was so far beyond the gulf that when they looked back they could not see it at all.

Cayke now got off the Frogman's back and he stood erect again and carefully brushed the dust from his velvet coat and rearranged his white satin necktie.

"I had no idea I could leap so far," he said wonderingly. "Leaping is one more accomplishment I can now add to the long list of deeds I am able to perform."

"You are certainly fine at leap-frog," said the Cookie Cook, admiringly; "but, as you say, you are wonderful in many ways. If we meet with any people down here I am sure they will consider you the greatest and grandest of all living creatures."

"Yes," he replied, "I shall probably astonish strangers, because they have never before had the pleasure of seeing me. Also they will marvel at my great learning. Every time I open my mouth, Cayke, I am liable to say something important."

"That is true," she agreed, "and it is fortunate your mouth is so very wide and opens so far, for

otherwise all the wisdom might not be able to get out of it."

"Perhaps nature made it wide for that very reason," said the Frogman. "But come; let us now go on, for it is getting late and we must find some sort of shelter before night overtakes us."

Among the Winkies

CHAPTER 4

THE settled parts of
the Winkie Country
are full of happy and
contented people who
are ruled by a tin Emperor named Nick
Chopper, who in turn is a subject of the beautiful girl Ruler, Ozma of Oz. But not all of the
Winkie Country is fully settled. At the east,
which part lies nearest the Emerald City, there
are beautiful farmhouses and roads, but as you
travel west you first come to a branch of the
Winkie River, beyond which there is a rough
country where few people live, and some of
these are quite unknown to the rest of the world.
After passing through this rude section of territory, which no one ever visits, you would come

to still another branch of the Winkie River, after crossing which you would find another well-settled part of the Winkie Country, extending westward quite to the Deadly Desert that surrounds all the Land of Oz and separates that favored fairyland from the more common outside world. The Winkies who live in this west section have many tin mines, from which metal they make a great deal of rich jewelry and other articles, all of which are highly esteemed in the Land of Oz because tin is so bright and pretty, and there is not so much of it as there is of gold and silver.

Not all the Winkies are miners, however, for some till the fields and grow grains for food, and it was at one of these far west Winkie farms that the Frogman and Cayke the Cookie Cook first arrived after they had descended from the mountain of the Yips.

"Goodness me!" cried Nellary, the Winkie wife, when she saw the strange couple approaching her house. "I have seen many queer creatures in the Land of Oz, but none more queer than this giant frog, who dresses like a man and walks on his hind legs. Come here, Wiljon," she called to her husband, who was eating his breakfast, "and take a look at this astonishing freak."

Wiljon the Winkie came to the door and

looked out. He was still standing in the doorway when the Frogman approached and said with a haughty croak:

"Tell me, my good man, have you seen a diamond-studded gold dishpan?"

"No; nor have I seen a copper-plated lobster," replied Wiljon, in an equally haughty tone.

The Frogman stared at him and said:

"Do not be insolent, fellow!"

"No," added Cayke the Cookie Cook, hastily, "you must be very polite to the great Frogman, for he is the wisest creature in all the world."

"Who says that?" inquired Wiljon.

"He says so himself," replied Cayke, and the Frogman nodded and strutted up and down, twirling his gold-headed cane very gracefully.

"Does the Scarecrow admit that this overgrown frog is the wisest creature in the world?" asked Wiljon.

"I do not know who the Scarecrow is," answered Cayke the Cookie Cook.

"Well, he lives at the Emerald City, and he is supposed to have the finest brains in all Oz. The Wizard gave them to him, you know."

"Mine grew in my head," said the Frogman pompously, "so I think they must be better than any wizard brains. I am so wise that sometimes my wisdom makes my head ache. I know so much that often I have to forget part of it, since

no one creature, however great, is able to contain so much knowledge."

"It must be dreadful to be stuffed full of wisdom," remarked Wiljon reflectively, and eyeing the Frogman with a doubtful look. "It is my good fortune to know very little."

"I hope, however, you know where my jeweled dishpan is," said the Cookie Cook anxiously.

"I do not know even that," returned the Winkie. "We have trouble enough in keeping track of our own dishpans, without meddling with the dishpans of strangers."

Finding him so ignorant, the Frogman proposed that they walk on and seek Cayke's dishpan elsewhere. Wiljon the Winkie did not seem greatly impressed by the great Frogman, which seemed to that personage as strange as it was disappointing; but others in this unknown land might prove more respectful.

"I'd like to meet that Wizard of Oz," remarked Cayke, as they walked along a path. "If he could give a Scarecrow brains he might be able to find my dishpan."

"Poof!" grunted the Frogman scornfully; "I am greater than any wizard. Depend on *me*. If your dishpan is anywhere in the world I am sure to find it."

"If you do not, my heart will be broken," declared the Cookie Cook in a sorrowful voice.

For a while the Frogman walked on in silence. Then he asked:

"Why do you attach so much importance to a dishpan?"

"It is the greatest treasure I possess," replied the woman. "It belonged to my mother and to all my grandmothers, since the beginning of time. It is, I believe, the very oldest thing in all the Yip Country—or was while it was there—and," she added, dropping her voice to an awed whisper, "it has magic powers!"

"In what way?" inquired the Frogman, seeming to be surprised at this statement.

"Whoever has owned that dishpan has been a good cook, for one thing. No one else is able to make such good cookies as I have cooked, as you and all the Yips know. Yet, the very morning after my dishpan was stolen. I tried to make a batch of cookies and they burned up in the oven! I made another batch that proved too tough to eat, and I was so ashamed of them that I buried them in the ground. Even the third batch of cookies, which I brought with me in my basket, were pretty poor stuff and no better than any woman could make who does not own my diamond-studded gold dishpan. In fact, my good Frogman, Cayke the Cookie Cook will never be able to cook good cookies again until her magic dishpan is restored to her."

"In that case," said the Frogman with a sigh, "I suppose we must manage to find it."

Ozma's Friends Are Perplexed

CHAPTER 5

"REALLY," said Dorothy, looking solemn, "this is very s'prising. We can't find even a shadow of Ozma anywhere in the Em'rald City; and, wherever she's gone, she's taken her Magic Picture with her."

She was standing in the courtyard of the palace with Betsy and Trot, while Scraps, the Patchwork Girl, danced around the group, her hair flying in the wind.

"P'raps," said Scraps, still dancing, "someone has stolen Ozma."

"Oh, they'd never dare do that!" exclaimed tiny Trot.

"And stolen the Magic Picture, too, so the

thing can't tell where she is," added the Patchwork Girl.

"That's nonsense," said Dorothy. "Why, ev'ry-one loves Ozma. There isn't a person in the Land of Oz who would steal a single thing she owns."

"Huh!" replied the Patchwork Girl. "You don't know ev'ry person in the Land of Oz."

"Why don't I?"

"It's a big country," said Scraps. "There are cracks and corners in it that even Ozma doesn't know of."

"The Patchwork Girl's just daffy," declared Betsy.

"No; she's right about that," replied Dorothy thoughtfully. "There are lots of queer people in this fairyland who never come near Ozma or the Em'rald City. I've seen some of 'em my-self, girls; but I haven't seen all, of course, and there *might* be some wicked persons left in Oz, yet, though I think the wicked witches have all been destroyed."

Just then the Wooden Sawhorse dashed into the courtyard with the Wizard of Oz on his back.

"Have you found Ozma?" cried the Wizard when the Sawhorse stopped beside them.

"Not yet," said Dorothy. "Doesn't Glinda know where she is?"

"No. Glinda's Book of Records and all her magic instruments are gone. Someone must have stolen them."

"Goodness me!" exclaimed Dorothy, in alarm. "This is the biggest steal I ever heard of. Who do you think did it, Wizard?"

"I've no idea," he answered. "But I have come to get my own bag of magic tools and carry them to Glinda. She is so much more powerful than I that she may be able to discover the truth by means of my magic, quicker and better than I could myself."

"Hurry, then," said Dorothy, "for we're all getting terr'bly worried."

The Wizard rushed away to his rooms but presently came back with a long, sad face.

"It's gone!" he said.

"What's gone?" asked Scraps.

"My black bag of magic tools. Someone must have stolen it!"

They looked at one another in amazement.

"This thing is getting desperate," continued the Wizard. "All the magic that belongs to Ozma, or to Glinda, or to me, has been stolen."

"Do you suppose Ozma could have taken them, herself, for some purpose?" asked Betsy.

"No, indeed," declared the Wizard. "I suspect some enemy has stolen Ozma and, for fear we would follow and recapture her, has taken all our magic away from us."

"How dreadful!" cried Dorothy. "The idea of anyone wanting to injure our dear Ozma! Can't we do *any*thing to find her, Wizard?"

"I'll ask Glinda. I must go straight back to her and tell her that my magic tools have also disappeared. The good Sorceress will be greatly shocked, I know."

With this he jumped upon the back of the Sawhorse again and the quaint steed, which never tired, dashed away at full speed.

The three girls were very much disturbed in mind. Even the Patchwork Girl was more quiet than usual and seemed to realize that a great calamity had overtaken them all. Ozma was a fairy of considerable power and all the creatures in Oz, as well as the three mortal girls from the outside world, looked upon her as their protector and friend. The idea of their beautiful girl Ruler's being overpowered by an enemy and dragged from her splendid palace a captive was too astonishing for them to comprehend, at first. Yet what other explanation of the mystery could there be?

"Ozma wouldn't go away willingly, without letting us know about it," asserted Dorothy; "and she wouldn't steal Glinda's Great Book of Records, or the Wizard's magic, 'cause she could get them any time, just asking for 'em. I'm sure some wicked person has done all this."

"Someone in the Land of Oz?" asked Trot.

"Of course. No one could get across the Deadly Desert, you know, and no one but an Oz person could know about the Magic Picture and the Book of Records and the Wizard's magic, or where they were kept, and so be able to steal the whole outfit before we could stop 'em. It *must* be someone who lives in the Land of Oz."

"But who—who—who?" asked Scraps. "That's the question. Who?"

"If we knew," replied Dorothy, severely, "we wouldn't be standing here, doing nothing."

Just then two boys entered the courtyard and approached the group of girls. One boy was dressed in the fantastic Munchkin costume—a blue jacket and knickerbockers, blue leather shoes and a blue hat with a high peak and tiny silver bells dangling from its rim—and this was Ojo the Lucky, who had once come from the Munchkin Country of Oz and now lived in the Emerald City. The other boy was an American, from Philadelphia, and had lately found his way to Oz in the company of Trot and Cap'n Bill. His name was Button-Bright; that is, everyone called him by that name, and knew no other.

Button-Bright was not quite as big as the Munchkin boy, but he wore the same kind of clothes, only they were of different colors. As the two came up to the girls, arm in arm, Button-Bright remarked:

"Hello, Dorothy. They say Ozma is lost."

"*Who* says so?" she asked.

"Ev'rybody's talking about it, in the City," he replied.

"I wonder how the people found it out?" Dorothy asked.

"I know," said Ojo. "Jellia Jamb told them. She has been asking everywhere if anyone has seen Ozma."

"That's too bad," observed Dorothy, frowning.

"Why?" asked Button-Bright.

"There wasn't any use making all our people unhappy, till we were dead certain that Ozma can't be found."

"Pshaw," said Button-Bright, "It's nothing to get lost. I've been lost lots of times."

"That's true," admitted Trot, who knew that the boy had a habit of getting lost and then finding himself again; "but it's diff'rent with Ozma. She's the Ruler of all this big fairyland and we're 'fraid that the reason she's lost is because somebody has stolen her away."

"Only wicked people steal," said Ojo. "Do you know of any wicked people in Oz, Dorothy?"

"No," she replied.

"They're here, though," cried Scraps, dancing up to them and then circling around the group. "Ozma's stolen; someone in Oz stole her; only wicked people steal; so someone in Oz is wicked!"

There was no denying the truth of this statement. The faces of all of them were now solemn and sorrowful.

"One thing is sure," said Button-Bright, after a time, "if Ozma has been stolen, someone ought to find her and punish the thief."

"There may be a lot of thieves," suggested Trot gravely, "and in this fairy country they don't seem to have any soldiers or policemen."

"There is one soldier," claimed Dorothy. "He has green whiskers and a gun and is a Major-General; but no one is afraid of either his gun or his whiskers, 'cause he's so tender-hearted that he wouldn't hurt a fly."

"Well, a soldier's a soldier," said Betsy, "and perhaps he'd hurt a wicked thief if he wouldn't hurt a fly. Where is he?"

"He went fishing about two months ago and hasn't come back yet," explained Button-Bright.

"Then I can't see that he will be of much use to us in this trouble," sighed little Trot. "But p'raps Ozma, who is a fairy, can get away from the thieves without any help from anybody."

"She *might* be able to," admitted Dorothy, reflectively, "but if she had the power to do that, it isn't likely she'd have let herself be stolen. So the thieves must have been even more powerful in magic than our Ozma."

There was no denying this argument and, although they talked the matter over all the rest of that day, they were unable to decide how Ozma had been stolen against her will or who had committed the dreadful deed.

Toward evening the Wizard came back, riding slowly upon the Sawhorse because he felt discouraged and perplexed. Glinda came, later, in her aerial chariot drawn by twenty milk-white swans, and she also seemed worried and unhappy. More of Ozma's friends joined them and that evening they all had a long talk together.

"I think," said Dorothy, "we ought to start out right away in search of our dear Ozma. It seems cruel for us to live comf'tably in her palace while she is a pris'ner in the power of some wicked enemy."

"Yes," agreed Glinda the Sorceress, "someone ought to search for her. I cannot go myself, because I must work hard in order to create some new instruments of sorcery by means of which I may rescue our fair Ruler. But if you can find her, in the meantime, and let me know who has stolen her, it will enable me to rescue her much more quickly."

"Then we'll start to-morrow morning," decided Dorothy. "Betsy and Trot and I won't waste another minute."

"I'm not sure you girls will make good detectives," remarked the Wizard; "but I'll go with you, to protect you from harm and to give you my advice. All my wizardry, alas, is stolen, so

I am now really no more a wizard than any of you; but I will try to protect you from any enemies you may meet."

"What harm could happen to us in Oz?" inquired Trot.

"What harm happened to Ozma?" returned the Wizard. "If there is an Evil Power abroad in our fairyland, which is able to steal not only Ozma and her Magic Picture, but Glinda's Book of Records and all her magic, and my black bag containing all my tricks of wizardry, then that Evil Power may yet cause us considerable injury. Ozma is a fairy, and so is Glinda, so no power can kill or destroy them; but you girls are all mortals, and so are Button-Bright and I, so we must watch out for ourselves."

"Nothing can kill me," said Ojo, the Munchkin boy.

"That is true," replied the Sorceress, "and I think it may be well to divide the searchers into several parties, that they may cover all the land of Oz more quickly. So I will send Ojo and Unc Nunkie and Dr. Pipt into the Munchkin Country, which they are well acquainted with; and I will send the Scarecrow and the Tin Woodman into the Quadling Country, for they are fearless and brave and never tire; and to the Gillikin Country, where many dangers lurk, I will send the Shaggy Man and his brother, with Tik-Tok and Jack Pumpkinhead. Dorothy may make up

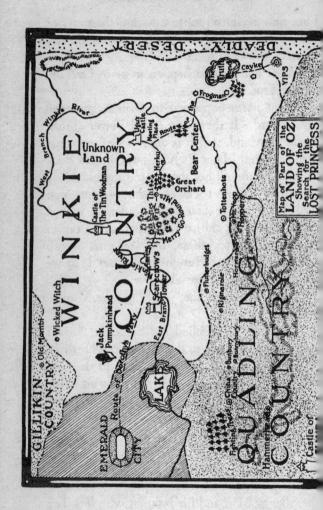

her own party and travel into the Winkie Country. All of you must inquire everywhere for Ozma and try to discover where she is hidden."

They thought this a very wise plan and adopted it without question. In Ozma's absence Glinda the Good was the most important person in Oz and all were glad to serve under her direction.

The Search Party

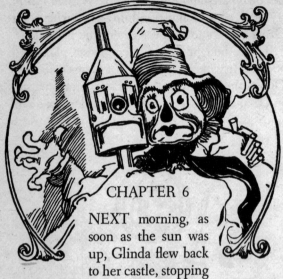

CHAPTER 6

NEXT morning, as soon as the sun was up, Glinda flew back to her castle, stopping on the way to instruct the Scarecrow and the Tin Woodman, who were at that time staying at the college of Professor H. M. Wogglebug, T. E., and taking a course of his Patent Educational Pills. On hearing of Ozma's loss they started at once for the Quadling Country to search for her.

As soon as Glinda had left the Emerald City, Tik-Tok and the Shaggy Man and Jack Pumpkinhead, who had been present at the conference, began their journey into the Gillikin Country, and an hour later Ojo and Unc Nunkie joined Dr. Pipt and together they traveled toward the Munchkin Country. When all these searchers were gone, Dorothy and the Wizard completed their own preparations.

The Wizard hitched the Sawhorse to the Red Wagon, which would seat four very comfortably. He wanted Dorothy, Betsy, Trot and the Patchwork Girl to ride in the wagon, but Scraps came up to them mounted upon the Woozy, and the Woozy said he would like to join the party. Now this Woozy was a most peculiar animal, having a square head, square body, square legs and square tail. His skin was very tough and hard, resembling leather, and while his movements were somewhat clumsy the beast could travel with remarkable swiftness. His square eyes were mild and gentle in expression and he was not especially foolish. The Woozy and the Patchwork Girl were great friends and so the Wizard agreed to let the Woozy go with them.

Another great beast now appeared and asked to go along. This was none other than the famous Cowardly Lion, one of the most interesting creatures in all Oz. No lion that roamed the jungles or plains could compare in size or intelligence with this Cowardly Lion, who—like all animals living in Oz—could talk, and who talked with more shrewdness and wisdom than many of the people did. He said he was cowardly because he always trembled when he faced danger, but he had faced danger many times and never

refused to fight when it was necessary. This Lion was a great favorite with Ozma and always guarded her throne on state occasions. He was also an old companion and friend of the Princess Dorothy, so the girl was delighted to have him join the party.

"I'm so nervous over our dear Ozma," said the Cowardly Lion in his deep, rumbling voice, "that it would make me unhappy to remain behind while you are trying to find her. But do not get into any danger, I beg of you, for danger frightens me terribly."

"We'll not get into danger if we can poss'bly help it," promised Dorothy; "but we shall do anything to find Ozma, danger or no danger."

The addition of the Woozy and the Cowardly Lion to the party gave Betsy Bobbin an idea and she ran to the marble stables at the rear of the palace and brought out her mule, Hank by name. Perhaps no mule you ever saw was so lean and bony and altogether plain looking as this Hank, but Betsy loved him dearly because he was faithful and steady and not nearly so stupid as most mules are considered to be. Betsy had a saddle for Hank and declared she would ride on his back, an arrangement approved by the Wizard because it left only four of the party to ride on the seats of the Red Wagon—Dorothy and Button-Bright and Trot and himself.

An old sailor-man, who had one wooden leg,

came to see them off and suggested that they put a supply of food and blankets in the Red Wagon, inasmuch as they were uncertain how long they would be gone. This sailor-man was called Cap'n Bill. He was a former friend and comrade of Trot and had encountered many adventures in company with the little girl. I think he was sorry he could not go with her on this trip, but Glinda the Sorceress had asked Cap'n Bill to remain in the Emerald City and take charge of the royal palace while everyone else was away, and the one-legged sailor had agreed to do so.

They loaded the back end of the Red Wagon with everything they thought they might need, and then they formed a procession and marched from the palace through the Emerald City to the great gates of the wall that surrounded this beautiful capital of the Land of Oz. Crowds of citizens lined the streets to see them pass and to cheer them and wish them success, for all were grieved over Ozma's loss and anxious that she be found again.

First came the Cowardly Lion; then the Patchwork Girl riding upon the Woozy; then Betsy Bobbin on her mule Hank; and finally the Sawhorse drawing the Red Wagon, in which were seated the Wizard and Dorothy and Button-Bright and Trot. No one was obliged to drive the Sawhorse, so there were no reins to his harness; one had only to tell him which way to go, fast or slow, and he understood perfectly.

It was about this time that a shaggy little black dog who had been lying asleep in Dorothy's room in the palace woke up and discovered he was lonesome. Everything seemed very still throughout the great building and Toto—that was the little dog's name—missed the customary chatter of the three girls. He never paid much attention to what was going on around him and, although he could speak, he seldom said anything; so the little dog did not know about Ozma's loss or that everyone had gone in search of her. But he liked to be with people, and especially with his own mistress, Dorothy, and having yawned and stretched himself and found the door of the room ajar he trotted out into the corridor and went down the stately marble stairs to the hall of the palace, where he met Jellia Jamb.

"Where's Dorothy?" asked Toto.

"She's gone to the Winkie Country," answered the maid.

"When?"

"A little while ago,' replied Jellia.

Toto turned and trotted out into the palace garden and down the long driveway until he came to the streets of the Emerald City. Here he paused to listen and, hearing sounds of cheering, he ran swiftly along until he came in sight of the Red Wagon and the Woozy and

the Lion and the Mule and all the others. Being a wise little dog, he decided not to show himself to Dorothy just then, lest he be sent back home; but he never lost sight of the party of travelers, all of whom were so eager to get ahead that they never thought to look behind them.

When they came to the gates in the city wall the Guardian of the Gates came out to throw wide the golden portals and let them pass through.

"Did any strange person come in or out of the city on the night before last, when Ozma was stolen?" asked Dorothy.

"No, indeed, Princess," answered the Guardian of the Gates.

"Of course not," said the Wizard. "Anyone clever enough to steal all the things we have lost would not mind the barrier of a wall like this, in the least. I think the thief must have flown through the air, for otherwise he could not have stolen from Ozma's royal palace and Glinda's far-away castle in the same night. Moreover, as there are no airships in Oz and no way for airships from the outside world to get into this country, I believe the thief must have flown from place to place by means of magic arts which neither Glinda nor I understand."

On they went, and before the gates closed behind them Toto managed to dodge through them. The country surrounding the Emerald

City was thickly settled and for a while our friends rode over nicely paved roads which wound through a fertile country dotted with beautiful houses, all built in the quaint Oz fashion. In the course of a few hours, however, they had left the tilled fields and entered the Country of the Winkies, which occupies a quarter of all the territory in the Land of Oz but is not so well known as many other parts of Ozma's fairyland. Long before night the travelers had crossed the Winkie River near to the Scarecrow's Tower (which was now vacant) and had entered the Rolling Prairie where few people live. They asked everyone they met for news of Ozma, but none in this district had seen her or even knew that she had been stolen. And by nightfall they had passed all the farmhouses and were obliged to stop and ask for shelter at the hut of a lonely shepherd. When they halted, Toto was not far behind. The little dog halted, too, and stealing softly around the party he hid himself behind the hut.

The shepherd was a kindly old man and treated the travelers with much courtesy. He slept out of doors, that night, giving up his hut to the three girls, who made their beds on the floor with the blankets they had brought in the Red Wagon. The Wizard and Button-Bright also slept out of doors, and so did the Cowardly Lion and Hank the Mule. But Scraps and the

Sawhorse did not sleep at all and the Woozy could stay awake for a month at a time, if he wished to, so these three sat in a little group by themselves and talked together all through the night.

In the darkness the Cowardly Lion felt a shaggy little form nestling beside his own, and he said sleepily:

"Where did you come from, Toto?"

"From home," said the dog. "If you roll over, roll the other way, so you won't smash me."

"Does Dorothy know you are here?" asked the Lion.

"I believe not," admitted Toto, and he added, a little anxiously: "Do you think, friend Lion, we are now far enough from the Emerald City for me to risk showing myself? Or will Dorothy send me back bacause I wasn't invited?"

"Only Dorothy can answer that question," said the Lion. "For my part, Toto, I consider this affair none of my business, so you must act as you think best."

Then the huge beast went to sleep again and Toto snuggled closer to his warm, hairy body and also slept. He was a wise little dog, in his way, and didn't intend to worry when there was something much better to do.

In the morning the Wizard built a fire, over which the girls cooked a very good breakfast.

Suddenly Dorothy discovered Toto sitting

quietly before the fire and the little girl exclaimed:

"Goodness me, Toto! Where did *you* come from?"

"From the place you cruelly left me," replied the dog in a reproachful tone.

"I forgot all about you," admitted Dorothy, "and if I hadn't I'd prob'ly left you with Jellia Jamb, seeing this isn't a pleasure trip but stric'ly business. But, now that you're here, Toto, I s'pose you'll have to stay with us, unless you'd rather go back home again. We may get ourselves into trouble, before we're done, Toto."

"Never mind that," said Toto, wagging his tail. "I'm hungry, Dorothy."

"Breakfas'll soon be ready and then you shall have your share," promised his little mistress, who was really glad to have her dog with her. She and Toto had traveled together before, and she knew he was a good and faithful comrade.

When the food was cooked and served the girls invited the old shepherd to join them in their morning meal. He willingly consented and while they ate he said to them:

"You are now about to pass through a very dangerous country, unless you turn to the north or to the south to escape its perils."

"In that case," said the Cowardly Lion, "let us turn, by all means, for I dread to face dangers of any sort."

"What's the matter with the country ahead of us?" inquired Dorothy.

"Beyond this Rolling Prairie," explained the shepherd, "are the Merry-Go-Round Mountains, set close together and surrounded by deep gulfs, so that no one is able to get past them. Beyond the Merry-Go-Round Mountains it is said the Thistle-Eaters and the Herkus live."

"What are they like?" demanded Dorothy.

"No one knows, for no one has ever passed the Merry-Go-Round Mountains," was the reply; "but it is said that the Thistle-Eaters hitch dragons to their chariots and that the Herkus are waited upon by giants whom they have conquered and made their slaves."

"Who says all that?" asked Betsy.

"It is common report," declared the shepherd. "Everyone believes it."

"I don't see how they know," remarked little Trot, "if no one has been there."

"Perhaps the birds who fly over that country brought the news," suggested Betsy.

"If you escaped those dangers," continued the shepherd, "you might encounter others, still more serious, before you came to the next branch of the Winkie River. It is true that beyond that river there lies a fine country, inhabited by good people, and if you reached there you would have no further trouble. It is between here and the west branch of the Winkie River that all dangers lie, for that is the unknown territory that is inhabited by terrible, lawless people."

"It may be, and it may not be," said the Wizard. "We shall know when we get there."

"Well," persisted the shepherd, "in a fairy country such as ours every undiscovered place is likely to harbor wicked creatures. If they were not wicked, they would discover themselves, and by coming among us submit to Ozma's rule and be good and considerate, as are all the Oz people whom we know."

"That argument," stated the little Wizard, "convinces me that it is our duty to go straight to those unknown places, however dangerous they may be; for it is surely some cruel and wicked person who has stolen our Ozma, and we know it would be folly to search among good people for the culprit. Ozma may not be hidden in the secret places of the Winkie Country, it is true, but it is our duty to travel to every spot, however dangerous, where our beloved Ruler is likely to be imprisoned."

"You're right about that," said Button-Bright approvingly. "Dangers don't hurt us; only things that happen ever hurt anyone, and a danger is a thing that might happen, and might not happen, and sometimes don't amount to shucks. I vote we go ahead and take our chances."

They were all of he same opinion, so they packed up and said good-bye to the friendly shepherd and proceeded on their way.

The Merry-Go-Round Mountains

CHAPTER 7

THE Rolling Prairie
was not difficult to
travel over, although
it was all up-hill and
down-hill, so for a while they made good progress. Not even a shepherd was to be met with
now and the farther they advanced the more
dreary the landscape became. At noon they
stopped for a "picnic luncheon," as Betsy called
it, and then they again resumed their journey.
All the animals were swift and tireless and even
the Cowardly Lion and the Mule found they
could keep up with the pace of the Woozy and
the Sawhorse.

It was the middle of the afternoon when first
they came in sight of a cluster of low mountains.
These were cone-shaped, rising from broad bases

to sharp peaks at the tops. From a distance the mountains appeared indistinct and seemed rather small—more like hills than mountains—but as the travelers drew nearer they noted a most unusual circumstance: the hills were all whirling around, some in one direction and some the opposite way.

"I guess those are the Merry-Go-Round Mountains, all right," said Dorothy.

"They must be," said the Wizard.

"They go 'round, sure enough," added Trot, "but they don't seem very merry."

There were several rows of these mountains, extending both to the right and to the left, for miles and miles. How many rows there might be, none could tell, but between the first row of peaks could be seen other peaks, all steadily whirling around one way or another. Continuing to ride nearer, our friends watched these hills attentively, until at last, coming close up, they discovered there was a deep but narrow gulf around the edge of each mountain, and that the mountains were set so close together that the outer gulf was continuous and barred farther advance.

At the edge of the gulf they all dismounted and peered over into its depths. There was no telling where the bottom was, if indeed there was any bottom at all. From where they stood it seemed as if the mountains had been set in one great hole in the ground, just close enough to-

gether so they would not touch, and that each
mountain was supported by a rocky column beneath its base which extended far down into the
black pit below. From the land side it seemed
impossible to get across the gulf or, succeeding
in that, to gain a foothold on any of the whirling
mountains.

"This ditch is too wide to jump across," remarked Button-Bright.

"P'raps the Lion could do it," suggested Dorothy.

"What, jump from here to that whirling hill?"
cried the Lion indignantly. "I should say not!
Even if I landed there, and could hold on, what
good would it do? There's another spinning
mountain beyond it, and perhaps still another
beyond that. I don't believe any living creature
could jump from one mountain to another, when
both are whirling like tops and in different
directions."

"I propose we turn back," said the Wooden
Sawhorse, with a yawn of his chopped-out
mouth, as he stared with his knot eyes at the
Merry-Go-Round Mountains.

"I agree with you," said the Woozy, wagging
his square head.

"We should have taken the shepherd's advice," added Hank the Mule.

The others of the party, however they might
be puzzled by the serious problem that con-

fronted them, would not allow themselves to despair.

"If we once get over these mountains," said Button-Bright, "we could probably get along all right."

"True enough," agreed Dorothy. "So we must find some way, of course, to get past these whirligig hills. But how?"

"I wish the Ork was with us," sighed Trot.

"But the Ork isn't here," said the Wizard, "and we must depend upon ourselves to conquer this difficulty. Unfortunately, all my magic has been stolen; otherwise I am sure I could easily get over the mountains."

"Unfortunately," observed the Woozy, "none of us has wings. And we're in a magic country without any magic."

"What is that around your waist, Dorothy?" asked the Wizard.

"That? Oh, that's just the Magic Belt I once captured from the Nome King," she replied.

"A Magic Belt! Why, that's fine. I'm sure a Magic Belt would take you over these hills."

"It might, if I knew how to work it," said the little girl. "Ozma knows a lot of its magic, but I've never found out about it. All I know is that while I am wearing it nothing can hurt me."

"Try wishing yourself across, and see if it will obey you," suggested the Wizard.

"But what good would that do?" asked Dorothy. "If I got across it wouldn't help the rest of you, and I couldn't go alone among all those giants and dragons, while you stayed here."

"True enough," agreed the Wizard, sadly; and then, after looking around the group, he inquired: "What is that on your finger, Trot?"

"A ring. The Mermaids gave it to me," she explained, "and if ever I'm in trouble when I'm on the water I can call the Mermaids and they'll come and help me. But the Mermaids can't help me on the land, you know, 'cause they swim, and—and—they haven't any legs."

"True enough," repeated the Wizard, more sadly.

There was a big, broad-spreading tree near the edge of the gulf and as the sun was hot above them they all gathered under the shade of the tree to study the problem of what to do next.

"If we had a long rope," said Betsy, "we could fasten it to this tree and let the other end of it down into the gulf and all slide down it."

"Well, what then?" asked the Wizard.

"Then, if we could manage to throw the rope up the other side," explained the girl, "we could all climb it and be on the other side of the gulf."

"There are too many 'if's' in that suggestion," remarked the little Wizard. "And you must remember that the other side is nothing but spinning mountains, so we couldn't possibly fasten a rope to them—even if we had one."

"That rope idea isn't half bad, though," said the Patchwork Girl, who had been dancing dangerously near to the edge of the gulf.

"What do you mean?" asked Dorothy.

The Patchwork Girl suddenly stood still and cast her button eyes around the group.

"Ha, I have it!" she exclaimed. "Unharness the Sawhorse, somebody; my fingers are too clumsy."

"Shall we?" asked Button-Bright doubtfully, turning to the others.

"Well, Scraps has a lot of brains, even if she *is* stuffed with cotton," asserted the Wizard. "If her brains can help us out of this trouble we ought to use them."

So he began unharnessing the Sawhorse, and Button-Bright and Dorothy helped him. When they had removed the harness the Patchwork Girl told them to take it all apart and buckle the straps together, end to end. And, after they had done this, they found they had one very long strap that was stronger than any rope.

"It would reach across the gulf, easily," said the Lion, who with the other animals had sat on his haunches and watched this proceeding. "But I don't see how it could be fastened to one of those dizzy mountains."

Scraps had no such notion as that in her baggy head. She told them to fasten one end of the strap to a stout limb of the tree, pointing to one which extended quite to the edge of the gulf. Button-Bright did that, climbing the tree and then crawling out upon the limb until he was nearly over the gulf. There he managed to fasten the strap, which reached to the ground below, and then he slid down it and was caught by the Wizard, who feared he might fall into the chasm.

Scraps was delighted. She seized the lower end of the strap and telling them all to get out of her way she went back as far as the strap would reach and then made a sudden run toward the gulf. Over the edge she swung, clinging to the strap until it had gone as far as its length permitted, when she let go and sailed gracefully through the air until she alighted upon the mountain just in front of them.

Almost instantly, as the great cone continued to whirl, she was sent flying against the next mountain in the rear, and that one had only turned halfway around when Scraps was sent flying to the next mountain behind it. Then her patchwork form disappeared from view entirely and the amazed watchers under the tree wondered what had become of her.

"She's gone, and she can't get back," said the Woozy.

"My, how she bounded from one mountain to another!" exclaimed the Lion.

"That was because they whirl so fast," the

Wizard explained. "Scraps had nothing to hold on to and so of course she was tossed from one hill to another. I'm afraid we shall never see the poor Patchwork Girl again."

"*I* shall see her," declared the Woozy. "Scraps is an old friend of mine and, if there are really Thistle-Eaters and Giants on the other side of those tops, she will need someone to protect her. So, here I go!"

He seized the dangling strap firmly in his square mouth and in the same way that Scraps had done swung himself over the gulf. He let go the strap at the right moment and fell upon the first whirling mountain. Then he bounded to the next one back of it—not on his feet but "all mixed up," as Trot said—and then he shot across to another mountain, disappearing from view just as the Patchwork Girl had done.

"It seems to work, all right," remarked Button-Bright. "I guess I'll try it."

"Wait a minute," urged the Wizard. "Before any more of us make this desperate leap into the beyond, we must decide whether all will go, or if some of us will remain behind."

"Do you s'pose it hurt them much, to bump against those mountains?" asked Trot.

"I don't s'pose anything could hurt Scraps or the Woozy," said Dorothy, "and nothing can hurt *me*, because I wear the Magic Belt. So, as

I'm anxious to find Ozma, I mean to swing myself across, too."

"I'll take my chances," decided Button-Bright.

"I'm sure it will hurt dreadfully, and I'm afraid to do it," said the Lion, who was already trembling; "but I shall do it if Dorothy does."

"Well, that will leave Betsy and the Mule and Trot," said the Wizard; "for of course, I shall go, that I may look after Dorothy. Do you two girls think you can find your way back home again?" he asked, addressing Trot and Betsy.

"I'm not afraid; not much, that is," said Trot. "It looks risky, I know, but I'm sure I can stand it if the others can."

"If it wasn't for leaving Hank," began Betsy, in a hesitating voice; but the Mule interrupted her by saying:

"Go ahead, if you want to, and I'll come after you. A mule is as brave as a lion, any day."

"Braver," said the Lion, "for I'm a coward, friend Hank, and you are not. But of course the Sawhorse—"

"Oh, nothing ever hurts *me*," asserted the Sawhorse calmly. "There's never been any question about *my* going. I can't take the Red Wagon, though."

"No, we must leave the wagon," said the Wizard; "and also we must leave our food and blankets, I fear. But if we can defy these Merry-

Go-Round Mountains to stop us we won't mind the sacrifice of some of our comforts."

"No one knows where we're going to land!" remarked the Lion, in a voice that sounded as if he were going to cry.

"We may not land at all," replied Hank; "but the best way to find out what will happen to us is to swing across, as Scraps and the Woozy have done."

"I think I shall go last," said the Wizard; "so who wants to go first?"

"I'll go," decided Dorothy.

"No, it's my turn first," said Button-Bright. "Watch me!"

Even as he spoke the boy seized the strap and after making a run swung himself across the gulf. Away he went, bumping from hill to hill until he disappeared. They listened intently, but the boy uttered no cry until he had been gone some moments, when they heard a faint "Hullo-a!" as if called from a great distance.

The sound gave them courage, however, and Dorothy picked up Toto and held him fast under one arm while with the other hand she seized the strap and bravely followed after Button-Bright.

When she struck the first whirling mountain she fell upon it quite softly, but before she had time to think she flew through the air and lit with a jar on the side of the next mountain.

Again she flew, and alighted; and again, and
still again, until after five successive bumps she
fell sprawling upon a green meadow and was
so dazed and bewildered by her bumpy journey
across the Merry-Go-Round Mountains that she
lay quite still for a time, to collect her thoughts.
Toto had escaped from her arms just as she fell,
and he now sat beside her panting with excitement.

Then Dorothy realized that someone was help-
ing her to her feet, and here was Button-Bright
on one side of her and Scraps on the other, both
seeming to be unhurt. The next object her eyes
fell upon was the Woozy, squatting upon his
square back end and looking at her reflectively,
while Toto barked joyously to find his mistress
unhurt after her whirlwind trip.

"Good!" said the Woozy; "here's another and
a dog, both safe and sound. But, my word,
Dorothy, you flew some! If you could have seen
yourself, you'd have been absolutely astonished."

"They say 'Time flies,' " laughed Button-
Bright; "but Time never made a quicker journey
than that."

Just then, as Dorothey turned around to look
at the whirling mountains, she was in time to
see tiny Trot come flying from the nearest hill
to fall upon the soft grass not a yard away from
where she stood. Trot was so dizzy she couldn't
stand, at first, but she wasn't at all hurt and

presently Betsy came flying to them and would have bumped into the others had they not retreated in time to avoid her.

Then, in quick succession, came the Lion, Hank and the Sawhorse, bounding from mountain to mountain to fall safely upon the greensward. Only the Wizard was now left behind and they waited so long for him that Dorothy began to be worried. But suddenly he came flying from the nearest mountain and tumbled heels over head beside them. Then they saw that he had wound two of their blankets around his body, to keep the bumps from hurting him, and had fastened the blankets with some of the spare straps from the harness of the Sawhorse.

The Mysterious City

CHAPTER 8

THERE they sat upon the grass, their heads still swimming from their dizzy flights, and looked at one another in silent bewilderment. But presently, when assured that no one was injured, they grew more calm and collected and the Lion said with a sigh of relief:

"Who would have thought those Merry-Go-Round Mountains were made of rubber?"

"Are they really rubber?" asked Trot.

"They must be," replied the Lion, "for otherwise we would not have bounded so swiftly from one to another without getting hurt."

"That is all guesswork," declared the Wizard, unwinding the blankets from his body, "for none of us stayed long enough on the mountains to discover what they are made of. But where are we?"

"That's guesswork, too," said Scraps. "The shepherd said the Thistle-Eaters live this side of the mountains and are waited on by giants."

"Oh, no," said Dorothy; "it's the Herkus who have giant slaves, and the Thistle-Eaters hitch dragons to their chariots."

"How could they do that?" asked the Woozy. "Dragons have long tails, which would get in the way of the chariot wheels."

"And, if the Herkus have conquered the giants," said Trot, "they must be at least twice the size of giants. P'raps the Herkus are the biggest people in all the world!"

"Perhaps they are," assented the Wizard, in a thoughtful tone of voice. "And perhaps the shepherd didn't know what he was talking about. Let us travel on toward the west and discover for ourselves what the people of this country are like."

It seemed a pleasant enough country, and it was quite still and peaceful when they turned their eyes away from the silently whirling mountains. There were trees here and there and green bushes, while throughout the thick grass were scattered brilliantly colored flowers. About a mile away was a low hill that hid from them all the country beyond it, so they realized they could not tell much about the country until they had crossed the hill.

The Red Wagon having been left behind, it was now necessary to make other arrangements for traveling. The Lion told Dorothy she could ride upon his back, as she had often done before, and the Woozy said he could easily carry both Trot and the Patchwork Girl. Betsy still had her mule, Hank, and Button-Bright and the Wizard could sit together upon the long, thin back of the Sawhorse, but they took care to soften their seat with a pad of blankets before they started. Thus mounted, the adventurers started for the hill, which was reached after a brief journey.

As they mounted the crest and gazed beyond the hill they discovered not far away a walled city, from the towers and spires of which gay banners were flying. It was not a very big city, indeed, but its walls were very high and thick and it appeared that the people who lived there must have feared attack by a powerful enemy, else they would not have surrounded their dwellings with so strong a barrier.

There was no path leading from the mountains to the city, and this proved that the people seldom or never visited the whirling hills; but our friends found the grass soft and agreeable to travel over and with the city before them they could not lose their way. When they drew

nearer to the walls, the breeze carried to their ears the sound of music—dim at first but growing louder as they advanced.

"That doesn't seem like a very terr'ble place," remarked Dorothy.

"Well, it *looks* all right," replied Trot, from her seat on the Woozy, "but looks can't always be trusted."

"*My* looks can," said Scraps. "I *look* patchwork, and I *am* patchwork, and no one but a blind owl could ever doubt that I'm the Patchwork Girl." Saying which she turned a somersault off the Woozy and, alighting on her feet, began wildly dancing about.

"Are owls ever blind?" asked Trot.

"Always, in the daytime," said Button-Bright. "But Scraps can see with her button eyes both day and night. Isn't it queer?"

"It's queer that buttons can see at all," answered Trot; "but—good gracious! what's become of the city?"

"I was going to ask that myself," said Dorothy. "It's gone!"

The animals came to a sudden halt, for the city had really disappeared—walls and all—and before them lay the clear, unbroken sweep of the country.

"Dear me!" exclaimed the Wizard. "This is rather disagreeable. It is annoying to travel almost to a place and then find it is not there."

"Where can it be, then?" asked Dorothy. "It cert'nly was there a minute ago."

"I can hear the music yet," declared Button-Bright, and when they all listened the strains of music could plainly be heard.

"Oh! there's the city—over at the left," called Scraps, and turning their eyes they saw the walls and towers and fluttering banners far to the left of them.

"We must have lost our way," suggested Dorothy.

"Nonsense," said the Lion. "I, and all the other animals, have been tramping straight toward the city ever since we first saw it."

"Then how does it happen—"

"Never mind," interrupted the Wizard, "we are no farther from it than we were before. It is in a different direction, that's all; so let us hurry and get there before it again escapes us."

So on they went, directly toward the city, which seemed only a couple of miles distant; but when they had traveled less than a mile it suddenly disappeared again. Once more they paused, somewhat discouraged, but in a moment the button eyes of Scraps again discovered the city, only this time it was just behind them, in the direction from which they had come.

"Goodness gracious!" cried Dorothy. "There's surely something wrong with that city. Do you s'pose it's on wheels, Wizard?"

"It may not be a city at all," he replied, looking toward it with a speculative gaze.

"What *could* it be, then?"

"Just an illusion."

"What's that?" asked Trot.

"Something you think you see and don't see."

"I can't believe that," said Button-Bright. "If we only saw it, we might be mistaken, but if we can see it and hear it, too, it must be there."

"Where?" asked the Patchwork Girl.

"Somewhere near us," he insisted.

"We will have to go back, I suppose," said the Woozy, with a sigh.

So back they turned and headed for the walled city until it disappeared again, only to reappear at the right of them. They were constantly getting nearer to it, however, so they kept their faces turned toward it as it flitted here and there to all points of the compass. Presently the Lion, who was leading the procession, halted abruptly and cried out: "Ouch!"

"What's the matter?" asked Dorothy.

"Ouch—ouch!" repeated the Lion, and leaped backward so suddenly that Dorothy nearly tumbled from his back. At the same time Hank the Mule yelled "Ouch!" almost as loudly as the Lion had done, and he also pranced backward a few paces.

"It's the thistles," said Betsy. "They prick their legs."

Hearing this, all looked down, and sure enough the ground was thick with thistles, which covered the plain from the point where they stood way up to the walls of the mysterious city. No pathways through them could be seen at all; here the soft grass ended and the growth of thistles began.

"They're the prickliest thistles I ever felt," grumbled the Lion. "My legs smart yet from their stings, though I jumped out of them as quick as I could."

"Here is a new difficulty," remarked the Wizard in a grieved tone. "The city has stopped hopping around, it is true; but how are we to get to it, over this mass of prickers?"

"They can't hurt *me*," said the thick-skinned Woozy, advancing fearlessly and trampling among the thistles.

"Nor me," said the Wooden Sawhorse.

"But the Lion and the Mule cannot stand the prickers," asserted Dorothy, "and we can't leave them behind."

"Must we all go back?" asked Trot.

"Course not!" replied Button-Bright scornfully. "Always, when there's trouble, there's a way out of it, if you can find it."

"I wish the Scarecrow was here," said Scraps, standing on her head on the Woozy's square back. "His splendid brains would soon show us how to conquer this field of thistles."

"What's the matter with *your* brains?" asked the boy.

"Nothing," she said, making a flip-flop into the thistles and dancing among them without feeling their sharp points. "I could tell you in half a minute how to get over the thistles, if I wanted to."

"Tell us, Scraps!" begged Dorothy.

"I don't want to wear my brains out with overwork," replied the Patchwork Girl.

"Don't you love Ozma? And don't you want to find her?" asked Betsy reproachfully.

"Yes, indeed," said Scraps, walking on her hands as an acrobat does at the circus.

"Well, we can't find Ozma unless we get past these thistles," declared Dorothy.

Scraps danced around them two or three times, without reply. Then she said:

"Don't look at me, you stupid folks; look at those blankets."

The Wizard's face brightened at once.

"Of course!" he exclaimed. "Why didn't we think of those blankets before?"

"Because you haven't magic brains," laughed Scraps. "Such brains as you have are of the common sort that grow in your heads, like weeds in a garden. I'm sorry for you people who have to be born in order to be alive."

But the Wizard was not listening to her. He quickly removed the blankets from the back of the Sawhorse and spread one of them upon the thistles, just next to the grass. The thick cloth rendered the prickers harmless, so the Wizard walked over this first blanket and spread the second one farther on, in the direction of the phantom city.

"These blankets," said he, "are for the Lion and the Mule to walk upon. The Sawhorse and the Woozy can walk on the thistles."

So the Lion and the Mule walked over the first blanket and stood upon the second one until the Wizard had picked up the one they had passed over and spread it in front of them, when they advanced to that one and waited while the one behind them was again spread in front.

"This is slow work," said the Wizard, "but it will get us to the city after a while."

"The city is a good half mile away, yet," announced Button-Bright.

"And this is awful hard work for the Wizard," added Trot.

"Why couldn't the Lion ride on the Woozy's back?" asked Dorothy. "It's a big, flat back, and the Woozy's mighty strong. Perhaps the Lion wouldn't fall off."

"You may try it, if you like," said the Woozy to the Lion. "I can take you to the city in a jiffy and then come back for Hank."

"I'm—I'm afraid," said the Cowardly Lion. He was twice as big as the Woozy.

"Try it," pleaded Dorothy.

"And take a tumble among the thistles?" asked the Lion reproachfully. But when the Woozy came close to him the big beast suddenly bounded upon its back and managed to balance himself there, although forced to hold his four legs so close together that he was in danger of toppling over. The great weight of the monster Lion did not seem to affect the Woozy, who called to his rider: "Hold on tight!" and ran swiftly over the thistles toward the city.

The others stood on the blankets and watched the strange sight anxiously. Of course the Lion couldn't "hold on tight" because there was nothing to hold to, and he swayed from side to side as if likely to fall off any moment. Still, he managed to stick to the Woozy's back until they were close to the walls of the city, when he leaped to the ground. Next moment the Woozy came dashing back at full speed.

"There's a little strip of ground next to the wall where there are no thistles," he told them, when he had reached the adventurers once more. "Now, then, friend Hank, see if you can ride as well as the Lion did."

"Take the others first," proposed the Mule. So the Sawhorse and the Woozy made a couple of trips over the thistles to the city walls and carried all the people in safety, Dorothy holding little Toto in her arms. The travelers then sat in a group on a little hillock, just outside the wall, and looked at the great blocks of gray stone and waited for the Woozy to bring Hank to them. The Mule was very awkward and his legs trembled so badly that more than once they thought he would tumble off, but finally he reached them in safety and the entire party was now reunited. More than that, they had reached the city that had eluded them for so long and in so strange a manner.

"The gates must be around the other side," said the Wizard. "Let us follow the curve of the wall until we reach an opening in it."

"Which way?" asked Dorothy.

"We must guess at that," he replied. "Suppose we go to the left? One direction is as good as another."

They formed in marching order and went around the city wall to the left. It wasn't a big city, as I have said, but to go way around it, outside the high wall, was quite a walk, as they became aware. But around it our adventurers went, without finding any sign of a gateway or other opening. When they had returned to the little mound from which they had started, they dismounted from the animals and again seated themselves on the grassy mound.

"It's mighty queer, isn't it?" asked Button-Bright.

"There must be *some* way for the people to

get out and in," declared Dorothy. "Do you s'pose they have flying machines, Wizard?"

"No," he replied, "for in that case they would be flying all over the Land of Oz, and we know they have not done that. Flying machines are unknown here. I think it more likely that the people use ladders to get over the walls."

"It would be an awful climb, over that high stone wall," said Betsy.

"Stone, is it?" cried Scraps, who was again dancing wildly around, for she never tired and could never keep still for long.

"Course it's stone," answered Betsy scornfully. "Can't you see?"

"Yes," said Scraps, going closer, "I can *see* the wall, but I can't *feel* it." And then, with her arms outstretched, she did a very queer thing. She walked right into the wall and disappeared.

"For goodness sake!" cried Dorothy amazed, as indeed they all were.

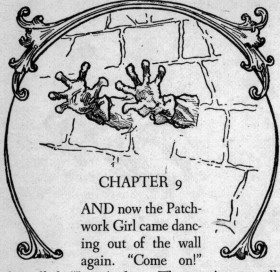

CHAPTER 9

AND now the Patch-
work Girl came danc-
ing out of the wall
again. "Come on!"
she called. "It isn't there. There isn't any wall
at all."

"What! No wall?" exclaimed the Wizard.

"Nothing like it," said Scraps. "It's a make-
believe. You see it, but it isn't. Come on into the
city; we've been wasting time."

With this she danced into the wall again and
once more disappeared. Button-Bright, who was
rather venturesome, dashed away after her and
also became invisible to them. The others followed more cautiously, stretching out their hands
to feel the wall and finding, to their astonishment, that they could feel nothing because noth-

ing opposed them. They walked on a few steps and found themselves in the streets of a very beautiful city. Behind them they again saw the wall, grim and forbidding as ever; but now they knew it was merely an illusion, prepared to keep strangers from entering the city.

But the wall was soon forgotten, for in front of them were a number of quaint people who stared at them in amazement, as if wondering where they had come from. Our friends forgot their good manners, for a time, and returned the stares with interest, for so remarkable a people had never before been discovered in all the remarkable Land of Oz.

Their heads were shaped like diamonds and their bodies like hearts. All the hair they had was a little bunch at the tip top of their diamond-shaped heads and their eyes were very large and round and their noses and mouths very small. Their clothing was tight-fitting and of brilliant colors, being handsomely embroidered in quaint designs with gold or silver threads; but on their feet they wore sandals, with no stockings whatever. The expression of their faces was pleasant enough, although they now showed surprise at the appearance of strangers so unlike themselves, and our friends thought they seemed quite harmless.

"I beg your pardon," said the Wizard, speaking for his party, "for intruding upon you uninvited, but we are traveling on important business and find it necessary to visit your city. Will you kindly tell us by what name your city is called?"

They looked at one another uncertainly, each expecting some other to answer. Finally a short one whose heart-shaped body was very broad replied:

"We have no occasion to call our city anything. It is where we live, that is all."

"But by what name do others call your city?" asked the Wizard.

"We know of no others, except yourselves," said the man. And then he inquired: "Were you born with those queer forms you have, or has some cruel magician transformed you to them from your natural shapes?"

"These are our natural shapes," declared the Wizard, "and we consider them very good shapes, too."

The group of inhabitants was constantly being enlarged by others who joined it. All were evidently startled and uneasy at the arrival of strangers.

"Have you a King?" asked Dorothy, who knew it was better to speak with someone in authority. But the man shook his diamond-like head.

"What is a King?" he asked.

"Isn't there anyone who rules over you?" in

quired the Wizard.

"No," was the reply, "each of us rules himself; or, at least, tries to do so. It is not an easy thing to do, as you probably know."

The Wizard reflected.

"If you have disputes among you," said he, after a little thought, "who settles them?"

"The High Coco-Lorum," they answered in a chorus.

"And who is he?"

"The judge who enforces the laws," said the man who had first spoken.

"Then he is the principal person here?" continued the Wizard.

"Well, I would not say that," returned the man in a puzzled way. "The High Coco-Lorum is a public servant. However, he represents the laws, which we must all obey."

"I think," said the Wizard, "we ought to see your High Coco-Lorum and talk with him. Our mission here requires us to consult one high in authority, and the High Coco-Lorum ought to be high, whatever else he is."

The inhabitants seemed to consider this proposition reasonable, for they nodded their diamond-shaped heads in approval. So the broad one who had been their spokesman said: "Follow me," and, turning, led the way along one of the streets.

The entire party followed him, the natives

falling in behind. The dwellings they passed were quite nicely planned and seemed comfortable and convenient. After leading them a few blocks their conductor stopped before a house which was neither better nor worse than the others. The doorway was shaped to admit the strangely formed bodies of these people, being narrow at the top, broad in the middle and tapering at the bottom. The windows were made in much the same way, giving the house a most peculiar appearance. When their guide opened the gate a music-box concealed in the gate-post began to play, and the sound attracted the attention of the High Coco-Lorum, who appeared at an open window and inquired:

"What has happened now?"

But in the same moment his eyes fell upon the strangers and he hastened to open the door and admit them—all but the animals, which were left outside with the throng of natives that had now gathered. For a small city there seemed to be a large number of inhabitants, but they did not try to enter the house and contented themselves with staring curiously at the strange animals. Toto followed Dorothy.

Our friends entered a large room at the front of the house, where the High Coco-Lorum asked them to be seated.

"I hope your mission here is a peaceful one,"

he said, looking a little worried, "for the Thists are not very good fighters and object to being conquered."

"Are your people called Thists?" asked Dorothy.

"Yes. I thought you knew that. And we call our city Thi."

"Oh!"

"We are Thists because we eat thistles, you know," continued the High Coco-Lorum.

"Do you really eat those prickly things?" inquired Button-Bright wonderingly.

"Why not?" replied the other. "The sharp points of the thistles cannot hurt us, because all our insides are gold-lined."

"Gold-lined!"

"To be sure. Our throats and stomachs are lined with solid gold, and we find the thistles nourishing and good to eat. As a matter of fact, there is nothing else in our country that is fit for food. All around the City of Thi grow countless thistles, and all we need do is to go and gather them. If we wanted anything else to eat we would have to plant it, and grow it, and harvest it, and that would be a lot of trouble and make us work, which is an occupation we detest."

"But, tell me, please," said the Wizard, "how does it happen that your city jumps around so, from one part of the country to another?"

"The city doesn't jump; it doesn't move at all," declared the High Coco-Lorum. "However, I will admit that the land that surrounds it has a trick of turning this way or that; and so, if one is standing upon the plain and facing north, he is likely to find himself suddenly facing west— or east—or south. But once you reach the thistle fields you are on solid ground."

"Ah, I begin to understand," said the Wizard, nodding his head. "But I have another question to ask: How does it happen that the Thists have no King to rule over them?"

"Hush!" whispered the High Coco-Lorum, looking uneasily around to make sure they were not overheard. "In reality, I am the King, but the people don't know it. They think they rule themselves, but the fact is I have everything my own way. No one else knows anything about our laws, and so I make the laws to suit myself. If any oppose me, or question my acts, I tell them it's the law, and that settles it. If I called myself King, however, and wore a crown and lived in royal state, the people would not like me, and might do me harm. As the High Coco-Lorum of Thi, I'm considered a very agreeable person."

"It seems a very clever arrangement," said the Wizard. "And now, as you are the principal person in Thi, I beg you to tell us if the Royal

Ozma is a captive in your city."

"No," answered the diamond-headed man, "we have no captives. No strangers but yourselves are here, and we have never before heard of the Royal Ozma."

"She rules all of Oz," said Dorothy, "and so she rules your city and you, because you are in the Winkie Country, which is a part of the Land of Oz."

"It may be," returned the High Coco-Lorum, "for we do not study geography and have never inquired whether we live in the Land of Oz or not. And any Ruler who rules us from a distance, and unknown to us, is welcome to the job. But what has happened to your Royal Ozma?"

"Someone has stolen her," said the Wizard. "Do you happen to have any talented magician among your people—one who is especially clever, you know?"

"No, none especially clever. We do some magic, of course, but it is all of the ordinary kind. I do not think any of us has yet aspired to stealing Rulers, either by magic or otherwise."

"Then we've come a long way for nothing!" exclaimed Trot regretfully.

"But we are going farther than this," asserted the Patchwork Girl, bending her stuffed body backward until her yarn hair touched the floor and then walking around on her hands with

her feet in the air.

The High Coco-Lorum watched Scraps admiringly.

"You may go farther on, of course," said he, "but I advise you not to. The Herkus live back of us, beyond the thistles and the twisting lands, and they are not very nice people to meet, I assure you."

"Are they giants?" asked Betsy.

"They are worse than that," was the reply. "They have giants for their slaves and they are so much stronger than giants that the poor slaves dare not rebel, for fear of being torn to pieces."

"How do you know?" asked Scraps.

"Everyone says so," answered the High Coco-Lorum.

"Have you seen the Herkus yourself?" inquired Dorothy.

"No, but what everyone says must be true; otherwise, what would be the use of their saying it?"

"We were told, before we got here, that you people hitch dragons to your chariots," said the little girl.

"So we do," declared the High Coco-Lorum. "And that reminds me that I ought to entertain you, as strangers and my guests, by taking you for a ride around our splendid City of Thi."

Coco-Lorum. "Every time I give an order it is in music, which is a much more pleasant way to address servants than in cold, stern words."

"Does this dragon of yours bite?" asked Button-Bright.

"Mercy, no! Do you think I'd risk the safety of my innocent people by using a biting dragon to draw my chariot? I'm proud to say that my dragon is harmless—unless his steering-gear breaks—and he was manufactured at the famous dragon-factory in this City of Thi. Here he comes and you may examine him for yourselves."

They heard a low rumble and a shrill squeaking sound and, going out to the front of the house, they saw coming around the corner a car drawn by a gorgeous jeweled dragon, which moved its head to right and left and flashed its eyes like the headlights of an automobile and uttered a growling noise as it slowly moved toward them.

When it stopped before the High Coco-Lorum's house Toto barked sharply at the sprawling beast, but even tiny Trot could see that the dragon was not alive. Its scales were of gold and each one was set with sparkling jewels, while it walked in such a stiff, regular manner that it could be nothing else than a machine. The chariot that trailed behind it was likewise of gold and jewels, and when they entered it they each one was set with sparkling jewels, while it walked in such a stiff, regular manner that it could be nothing else than a machine. The chariot that trailed behind it was likewise of gold and jewels, and when they entered it they found there were no seats. Everyone was supposed to stand up while riding.

The charioteer was a little diamond-headed fellow who straddled the neck of the dragon and moved the levers that made it go.

"This," said the High Coco-Lorum, pompously, "is a wonderful invention. We are all very proud of our auto-dragons, many of which are in use by our wealthy inhabitants. Start the thing going, charioteer!"

The charioteer did not move.

"You forgot to order him in music," suggested Dorothy.

"Ah, so I did." He touched a button and a music-box in the dragon's head began to play a tune. At once the little charioteer pulled over a lever and the dragon began to move—very slowly and groaning dismally as it drew the clumsy chariot after it. Toto trotted between the wheels. The Sawhorse, the Mule, the Lion and the Woozy followed after and had no trouble in keeping up with the machine; indeed, they had to go slow to keep from running into it. When the wheels turned another music-box concealed somewhere under the chariot played a lively march tune which was in striking contrast with the dragging movement of the strange vehicle and Button-Bright decided that the music he had heard when they first sighted this city was nothing else than a chariot plodding its weary way through the streets.

All the travelers from the Emerald City thought this ride the most uninteresting and dreary they had ever experienced, but the High Coco-Lorum seemed to think it was grand. He pointed out the different buildings and parks and fountains, in much the same way that the conductor of an American "sight-seeing wagon" does, and being guests they were obliged to submit to the ordeal. But they became a little worried when their host told them he had ordered a banquet prepared for them in the City Hall.

"What are we going to eat?" asked Button-Bright suspiciously.

"Thistles," was the reply; "fine, fresh thistles, gathered this very day."

Scraps laughed, for she never ate anything, but Dorothy said in a protesting voice:

"*Our* insides are not lined with gold, you know."

"How sad!" exclaimed the High Coco-Lorum; and then he added, as an afterthought: "But we can have the thistles boiled, if you prefer."

"I'm 'fraid they wouldn't taste good, even then," said little Trot. "Haven't you anything else to eat?"

The High Coco-Lorum shook his diamond-shaped head.

"Nothing that I know of," said he. "But why should we have anything else, when we have so many thistles? However, if you can't eat what we eat, don't eat anything. We shall not be offended and the banquet will be just as merry and delightful."

Knowing his companions were all hungry the Wizard said:

"I trust you will excuse us from the banquet, sir, which will be merry enough without us, although it is given in our honor. For, as Ozma is not in your city, we must leave here at once and seek her elsewhere."

"Sure we must!" agreed Dorothy, and she whispered to Betsy and Trot: "I'd rather starve somewhere else than in this city, and—who knows?—we may run across somebody who eats reg'lar food and will give us some."

So, when the ride was finished, in spite of the protests of the High Coco-Lorum they insisted on continuing their journey.

"It will soon be dark," he objected.

"We don't mind the darkness," replied the Wizard.

"Some wandering Herku may get you."

"Do you think the Herkus would hurt us?" asked Dorothy.

"I cannot say, not having the honor of their acquaintance. But they are said to be so strong that, if they had any other place to stand upon, they could lift the world."

"All of them together?" asked Button-Bright wonderingly.

"Any one of them could do it," said the High Coco Lorum.

"Have you heard of any magicians being among them?" asked the Wizard, knowing that only a magician could have stolen Ozma in the way she had been stolen.

"I am told it is quite a magical country," declared the High Coco-Lorum, "and magic is usually performed by magicians. But I have never heard that they have any invention or sorcery to equal our wonderful auto-dragons."

They thanked him for his courtesy and, mounting their own animals, rode to the farther side of the city and right through the Wall of Illusion out into the open country.

"I'm glad we got away so easily," said Betsy. "I didn't like those queer-shaped people."

"Nor did I," agreed Dorothy. "It seems dreadful to be lined with sheets of pure gold and have nothing to eat but thistles."

"They seemed happy and contented, though,"

remarked the little Wizard, "and those who are contented have nothing to regret and nothing more to wish for."

Toto Loses Something

CHAPTER 10

FOR a while the travelers were constantly losing their direction, for beyond the thistle fields they again found themselves upon the turning-lands, which swung them around in such a freakish manner that first they were headed one way and then another. But by keeping the City of Thi constantly behind them the adventurers finally passed the treacherous turning-lands and came upon a stony country where no grass grew at all. There were plenty of bushes, however, and although it was now almost dark the girls discovered some delicious yellow berries growing upon the bushes, one taste of which set them all to picking as many as they could find. The berries relieved their pangs of hunger, for a time, and as it now became too dark to see anything they camped where they were.

The three girls lay down upon one of the blankets—all in a row—and then the Wizard covered them with the other blanket and tucked them in. Button-Bright crawled under the shelter of some bushes and was asleep in half a minute. The Wizard sat down with his back to a big stone and looked at the stars in the sky and thought gravely upon the dangerous adventure they had undertaken, wondering if they would ever be able to find their beloved Ozma again. The animals lay in a group by themselves, a little distance from the others.

"I've lost my growl!" said Toto, who had been very silent and sober all that day. "What do you suppose has become of it?"

"If you had asked me to keep track of your growl, I might be able to tell you," remarked the Lion sleepily. "But, frankly, Toto, I supposed you were taking care of it yourself."

"It's an awful thing to lose one's growl," said Toto, wagging his tail disconsolately. "What if you lost your roar, Lion? Wouldn't you feel terrible?"

"My roar," replied the Lion, "is the fiercest thing about me. I depend on it to frighten my enemies so badly that they won't dare to fight me."

"Once," said the Mule, "I lost my bray, so that I couldn't call to Betsy to let her know I was hungry. That was before I could talk, you know, for I had not yet come into the Land of Oz, and I found it was certainly very uncomfortable not to be able to make a noise."

"You make enough noise now," declared Toto. "But none of you has answered my question: Where is my growl?"

"You may search *me*," said the Woozy. "I don't care for such things myself."

"You snore terribly," asserted Toto.

"It may be," said the Woozy. "What one does when asleep one is not accountable for. I wish you would wake me up, some time when I'm snoring, and let me hear the sound. Then I can judge whether it is terrible or delightful."

"It isn't pleasant, I assure you," said the Lion, yawning.

"To me it seems wholly unnecessary," declared Hank the Mule.

"You ought to break yourself of the habit," said the Sawhorse. "You never hear me snore, because I never sleep. I don't even whinny, as those puffy meat horses do. I wish that whoever stole Toto's growl had taken the Mule's bray and the Lion's roar and the Woozy's snore at the same time."

"Do you think, then, that my growl was stolen?"

"You have never lost it before, have you?" inquired the Sawhorse.

"Only once, when I had a sore throat from barking too long at the moon."

"Is your throat sore now?" asked the Woozy.

"No," replied the dog.

"I can't understand," said Hank, "why dogs bark at the moon. They can't scare the moon, and the moon doesn't pay any attention to the bark. So why do dogs do it?"

"Were you ever a dog?" asked Toto.

"No, indeed," replied Hank. "I am thankful to say I was created a mule—the most beautiful of all beasts—and have always remained one."

The Woozy sat upon his square haunches to examine Hank with care.

"Beauty," said he, "must be a matter of taste. I don't say your judgment is bad, friend Hank, or that you are so vulgar as to be conceited. But if you admire big waggly ears, and a tail like a paint-brush, and hoofs big enough for an elephant, and a long neck and a body so skinny that one can count the ribs with one eye shut—if that's your idea of beauty, Hank—then either you or I must be much mistaken."

"You're full of edges," sneered the Mule. "If I were square, as you are, I suppose you'd think me lovely."

"Outwardly, dear Hank, I would," replied the Woozy. "But to be really lovely one must be

beautiful without and within."

The Mule couldn't deny this statement, so he gave a disgusted grunt and rolled over so that his back was toward the Woozy. But the Lion, regarding the two calmly with his great yellow eyes, said to the dog:

"My dear Toto, our friends have taught us a lesson in humility. If the Woozy and the Mule are indeed beautiful creatures, as they seem to think, you and I must be decidedly ugly."

"Not to ourselves," protested Toto, who was a shrewd little dog. "You and I, Lion, are fine specimens of our own races. I am a fine dog and you are a fine lion. Only in point of comparison, one with another, can we be properly judged, so I will leave it to the poor old Sawhorse to decide which is the most beautiful animal among us all. The Sawhorse is wood, so he won't be prejudiced and will speak the truth."

"I surely will," responded the Sawhorse, wagging his ears, which were chips set in his wooden head. "Are you all agreed to accept my judgment?"

"We are!" they declared, each one hopeful.

"Then," said the Sawhorse, "I must point out to you the fact that you are all meat creatures, who tire unless they sleep, and starve unless they eat, and suffer from thirst unless they drink. Such animals must be very imperfect, and imperfect creatures cannot be beautiful. Now, I am made of wood."

"You surely have a wooden head," said the Mule.

"Yes, and a wooden body and wooden legs—which are as swift as the wind and as tireless. I've heard Dorothy say that 'handsome is as handsome does,' and I surely perform my duties in a handsome manner. Therefore, if you wish my honest judgment, I will confess that among us all I am the most beautiful."

The Mule snorted and the Woozy laughed; Toto had lost his growl and could only look scornfully at the Sawhorse, who stood in his place unmoved. But the Lion stretched himself and yawned, saying quietly:

"Were we all like the Sawhorse we would all be Sawhorses, which would be too many of the kind; were we all like Hank, we would be a herd of mules; if like Toto, we would be a pack of dogs; should we all become the shape of the Woozy, he would no longer be remarkable for his unusual appearance. Finally, were you all like me, I would consider you so common that I would not care to associate with you. To be individual, my friends, to be different from others, is the only way to become distinguished from the common herd. Let us be glad, therefore, that we differ from one another in form and in disposition. Variety is the spice of life and we are various enough to enjoy one another's society; so let us be content."

"There is some truth in that speech," remarked Toto reflectively. "But how about my lost growl?"

"The growl is of importance only to you," responded the Lion, "so it is your business to worry over the loss, not ours. If you love us, do not inflict your burdens on us; be unhappy all by yourself."

"If the same person stole my growl who stole Ozma," said the little dog, "I hope we shall find him very soon and punish him as he deserves. He must be the most cruel person in all the world, for to prevent a dog from growling when it is his nature to growl is just as wicked, in my opinion, as stealing all the magic in Oz."

Button-Bright Loses Himself

CHAPTER 11

THE Patchwork Girl, who never slept and who could see very well in the dark, had wandered among the rocks and bushes all night long, with the result that she was able to tell some good news the next morning.

"Over the crest of the hill before us," she said, "is a big grove of trees of many kinds, on which all sorts of fruits grow. If you will go there you will find a nice breakfast awaiting you."

This made them eager to start, so as soon as the blankets were folded and strapped to the back of the Sawhorse they all took their places on the animals and set out for the big grove Scraps had told them of.

As soon as they got over the brow of the hill they discovered it to be a really immense orchard, extending for miles to the right and left of them. As their way led straight through the trees they hurried forward as fast as possible.

The first trees they came to bore quinces, which they did not like. Then there were rows of citron trees and then crab apples and afterward limes and lemons. But beyond these they found a grove of big golden oranges, juicy and sweet, and the fruit hung low on the branches, so they could pluck it easily.

They helped themselves freely and all ate oranges as they continued on their way. Then, a little farther along, they came to some trees bearing fine red apples, which they also feasted on, and the Wizard stopped here long enough to tie a lot of the apples in one end of a blanket.

"We do not know what will happen to us after we leave this delightful orchard," he said, "so I think it wise to carry a supply of apples with us. We can't starve as long as we have apples, you know."

Scraps wasn't riding the Woozy just now. She loved to climb the trees and swing herself by the branches from one tree to another. Some of the choicest fruit was gathered by the Patchwork Girl from the very highest limbs and tossed down to the others.

Suddenly Trot asked: "Where's Button-

Bright?" and when the others looked for him they found the boy had disappeared.

"Dear me!" cried Dorothy. "I guess he's lost again, and that will mean our waiting here until we can find him."

"It's a good place to wait," suggested Betsy, who had found a plum tree and was eating some of its fruit.

"How can you wait here, and find Button-Bright, at one and the same time?" inquired the Patchwork Girl, hanging by her toes on a limb just over the heads of the three mortal girls.

"Perhaps he'll come back here," answered Dorothy.

"If he tries that, he'll prob'ly lose his way," said Trot. "I've known him to do that, lots of times. It's losing his way that gets him lost."

"Very true," said the Wizard. "So all the rest of you must stay here while I go look for the boy."

"Won't *you* get lost, too?" asked Betsy.

"I hope not, my dear."

"Let *me* go," said Scraps, dropping lightly to the ground. "I can't get lost, and I'm more likely to find Button-Bright than any of you."

Without waiting for permission she darted away through the trees and soon disappeared from their view.

"Dorothy," said Toto, squatting beside his little mistress, "I've lost my growl."

"How did that happen?" she asked.

"I don't know," replied Toto. "Yesterday morning the Woozy nearly stepped on me and I tried to growl at him and found I couldn't growl a bit."

"Can you bark?" inquired Dorothy.

"Oh, yes, indeed!"

"Then never mind the growl," said she.

"But what will I do when I get home to the Glass Cat and the Pink Kitten?" asked the little dog in an anxious voice.

"They won't mind, if you can't growl at them, I'm sure," said Dorothy. "I'm sorry for you, of course, Toto, for it's just those things we can't do that we want to do most of all; but before we get back you may find your growl again."

"Do you think the person who stole Ozma stole my growl?"

Dorothy smiled.

"Perhaps, Toto."

"Then he's a scoundrel!" cried the little dog.

"Anyone who would steal Ozma is as bad as bad can be," agreed Dorothy, "and when we remember that our dear friend, the lovely Ruler of Oz, is lost, we ought not to worry over just a growl."

Toto was not entirely satisfied with this remark, for the more he thought upon his lost growl the more important his misfortune became. When no one was looking he went away among the trees and tried his best to growl—even a little bit—but could not manage to do so. All he could do was bark, and a bark cannot take the place of a growl, so he sadly returned to the others.

Now, Button-Bright had no idea that he was lost, at first. He had merely wandered from tree to tree, seeking the finest fruit, until he discovered he was alone in the great orchard. But that didn't worry him just then and seeing some apricot trees farther on he went to them; then he discovered some cherry trees; just beyond these were some tangerines.

"We've found 'most ev'ry kind of fruit but peaches," he said to himself, "so I guess there are peaches here, too, if I can find the trees."

He searched here and there, paying no attention to his way, until he found that the trees surrounding him bore only nuts. He put some walnuts in his pockets and kept on searching and at last—right among the nut trees—he came upon one solitary peach tree. It was a graceful, beautiful tree, but although it was thickly leaved it bore no fruit except one large, splendid peach, rosy-cheeked and fuzzy and just right to eat.

Button-Bright had some trouble getting that lonesome peach, for it hung far out of reach; but he climbed the tree nimbly and crept out on the branch on which it grew and after several trials, during which he was in danger of falling, he finally managed to pick it. Then he got back to the ground and decided the fruit was well worth his trouble. It was delightfully fragrant and when he bit into it he found it the most delicious morsel he had ever tasted.

"I really ought to divide it with Trot and Dorothy and Betsy," he said; "but p'rhaps there are plenty more in some other part of the orchard."

In his heart he doubted this statement, for this was a solitary peach tree, while all the other fruits grew upon many trees set close to one another; but that one luscious bite made him unable to resist eating the rest of it and soon the peach was all gone except the pit.

Button-Bright was about to throw this peach-pit away when he noticed that it was of pure gold. Of course this surprised him, but so many things in the Land of Oz were surprising that he did not give much thought to the golden peach-pit. He put it in his pocket, however, to show to the girls, and five minutes afterward had forgotten all about it.

For now he realized that he was far separated from his companions, and knowing that this would worry them and delay their journey, he began to shout as loud as he could. His voice did not penetrate very far among all those trees, and after shouting a dozen times and getting no answer he sat down on the ground and said:

"Well, I'm lost again. It's too bad, but I don't see how it can be helped."

As he leaned his back against a tree he looked up and saw a Bluefinch fly down from the sky and alight upon a branch just before him. The bird looked and looked at him. First it looked with one bright eye and then turned its head and looked at him with the other eye. Then, fluttering its wings a little, it said:

"Oho! so you've eaten the enchanted peach, have you?"

"Was it enchanted?" asked Button-Bright.

"Of course," replied the Bluefinch. "Ugu the Shoemaker did that."

"But why? And how was it enchanted? And what will happen to one who eats it?" questioned the boy.

"Ask Ugu the Shoemaker; he knows," said the bird, pruning its feathers with its bill.

"And who is Ugu the Shoemaker?"

"The one who enchanted the peach, and placed it here—in the exact center of the Great Orchard—so no one would ever find it. We birds didn't dare to eat it; we are too wise for that. But you are Button-Bright, from the Emerald City, and you—_you_—YOU ate the enchanted peach! You must explain to Ugu the Shoemaker why you did that."

And then, before the boy could ask any more questions, the bird flew away and left him alone.

Button-Bright was not much worried to find that the peach he had eaten was enchanted. It certainly had tasted very good and his stomach didn't ache a bit. So again he began to reflect upon the best way to rejoin his friends.

"Whichever direction I follow is likely to be the wrong one," he said to himself, "so I'd better stay just where I am and let *them* find *me*—if they can."

A White Rabbit came hopping through the orchard and paused a little way off to look at him.

"Don't be afraid," said Button-Bright; "I won't hurt you."

"Oh, I'm not afraid for myself," returned the White Rabbit. "It's you I'm worried about."

"Yes; I'm lost," said the boy.

"I fear you are, indeed," answered the Rabbit. "Why on earth did you eat the enchanted peach?"

The boy looked at the excited little animal thoughtfully.

"There were two reasons," he explained. "One reason was that I like peaches, and the other reason was that I didn't know it was enchanted."

"That won't save you from Ugu the Shoemaker," declared the White Rabbit and it scurried away before the boy could ask any more questions.

"Rabbits and birds," he thought, "are timid

creatures and seem afraid of this shoemaker—whoever he may be. If there was another peach half as good as that other, I'd eat it in spite of a dozen enchantments or a hundred shoemakers!"

Just then Scraps came dancing along and saw him sitting at the foot of the tree.

"Oh, here you are!" she said. "Up to your old tricks, eh? Don't you know it's impolite to get lost and keep everybody waiting for you? Come along, and I'll lead you back to Dorothy and the others."

Button-Bright rose slowly to accompany her.

"That wasn't much of a loss," he said cheerfully. "I haven't been gone half a day, so there's no harm done."

Dorothy, however, when the boy rejoined the party, gave him a good scolding.

"When we're doing such an important thing as searching for Ozma," said she, "it's naughty for you to wander away and keep us from getting on. S'pose she's a pris'ner—in a dungeon cell!—do you want to keep our dear Ozma there any longer than we can help?"

"If she's in a dungeon cell, how are you going to get her out?" inquired the boy.

"Never you mind; we'll leave that to the Wizard; he's sure to find a way."

The Wizard said nothing, for he realized that without his magic tools he could do no more than any other person. But there was no use reminding his companions of that fact; it might discourage them.

"The important thing just now," he remarked, "is to find Ozma; and, as our party is again happily reunited, I propose we move on."

As they came to the edge of the Great Orchard the sun was setting and they knew it would soon be dark. So it was decided to camp under the trees, as another broad plain was before them. The Wizard spread the blankets on a bed of soft leaves and presently all of them except Scraps and the Sawhorse were fast asleep. Toto snuggled close to his friend the Lion, and the Woozy snored so loudly that the Patchwork Girl covered his square head with her apron to deaden the sound.

The Czarover of Herku

CHAPTER 12

TROT wakened just as the sun rose and, slipping out of the blankets, went to the edge of the Great Orchard and looked across the plain. Something glittered in the far distance.

"That looks like another city," she said half aloud.

"And another city it is," declared Scraps, who had crept to Trot's side unheard, for her stuffed feet made no sound. "The Sawhorse and I made a journey in the dark, while you were all asleep, and we found over there a bigger city than Thi. There's a wall around it, too, but it has gates and plenty of pathways."

"Did you go in?" asked Trot.

"No, for the gates were locked and the wall was a real wall. So we came back here again. It isn't far to the city. We can reach it in two hours after you've had your breakfasts."

Trot went back and, finding the other girls now awake, told them what Scraps had said. So they hurriedly ate some fruit—there were plenty of plums and fijoas in this part of the orchard—and then they mounted the animals and set out upon the journey to the strange city. Hank the Mule had breakfasted on grass and the Lion had stolen away and found a breakfast to his liking; he never told what it was, but Dorothy hoped the little rabbits and the field mice had kept out of his way. She warned Toto not to chase birds and gave the dog some apple, with which he was quite content. The Woozy was as fond of fruit as of any other food, except honey, and the Sawhorse never ate at all.

Except for their worry over Ozma they were all in good spirits as they proceeded swiftly over the plain. Toto still worried over his lost growl, but like a wise little dog kept his worry to himself. Before long the city grew nearer and they could examine it with interest.

In outward appearance the place was more imposing than Thi, and it was a square city, with a square, four-sided wall around it and on each side was a square gate of burnished copper. Everything about the city looked solid and substantial; there were no banners flying and the towers that rose above the city wall seemed bare of any ornament whatever.

A path led from the fruit orchard directly to one of the city gates, showing that the inhabitants preferred fruit to thistles. Our friends followed this path to the gate, which they found fast shut. But the Wizard advanced and pounded upon it with his fist, saying in a loud voice: "Open!"

At once there rose above the great wall a row of immense heads, all of which looked down at them as if to see who was intruding. The size of these heads was astonishing and our friends at once realized that they belonged to giants, who were standing within the city. All had thick, bushy hair and whiskers, on some the hair being white and on others black or red or yellow, while the hair of a few was just turning gray, showing that the giants were of all ages. However fierce the heads might seem the eyes were mild in expression, as if the creatures had been long subdued, and their faces expressed patience rather than ferocity.

"What's wanted?" asked one old giant, in a low, grumbling voice.

"We are strangers and we wish to enter the city," replied the Wizard.

"Do you come in war or peace?" asked another.

"In peace, of course," retorted the Wizard, and he added impatiently: "Do we look like an army of conquest?"

"No," said the first giant who had spoken, "you look like innocent tramps; but one never can tell by appearances. Wait here until we report to our masters. No one can enter here without the permission of Vig, the Czarover."

"Who's that?" inquired Dorothy. But the heads had all bobbed down and disappeared behind the wall, so there was no answer.

They waited a long time before the gate rolled back with a rumbling sound and a loud voice cried: "Enter!" But they lost no time in taking advantage of the invitation.

On either side of the broad street that led into the city from the gate stood a row of huge giants —twenty of them on a side and all standing so close together that their elbows touched. They wore uniforms of blue and yellow and were armed with clubs as big around as tree-trunks. Each giant had around his neck a broad band of gold, riveted on, to show he was a slave.

As our friends entered, riding upon the Lion, the Woozy, the Sawhorse and the Mule, the giants half turned and walked in two files on either side of them, as if escorting them on their way. It looked to Dorothy as if all her party had been made prisoners, for even mounted on their animals their heads scarcely reached to the knees of the marching giants. The girls and Button-Bright were anxious to know what sort of a city they had entered, and what the people were like who had made these powerful creatures their slaves. Through the legs of the giants, as they walked, Dorothy could see rows of houses on each side the street and throngs of people standing on the sidewalks; but the people were of ordinary size and the only remarkable thing about them was the fact that they were dreadfully lean and thin. Between their skin and their bones there seemed to be little or no flesh, and they were mostly stoop-shouldered and weary looking, even to the little children.

More and more Dorothy wondered how and why the great giants had ever submitted to become slaves of such skinny, languid masters, but there was no chance to question anyone until they arrived at a big palace located in the heart of the city. Here the giants formed lines to the entrance and stood still while our friends rode into the courtyard of the palace. Then the gates closed behind them and before them was a skinny little man who bowed low and said in a sad voice:

"If you will be so obliging as to dismount, it will give me pleasure to lead you into the presence of the World's Most Mighty Ruler, Vig the Czarover."

"I don't believe it!" said Dorothy indignantly.

"What don't you believe?" asked the man.

"I don't believe your Czarover can hold a candle to our Ozma."

"He wouldn't hold a candle under any circumstances, or to any living person," replied the man very seriously, "for he has slaves to do such things and the Mighty Vig is too dignified to do anything that others can do for him. He even obliges a slave to sneeze for him, if ever he catches cold. However, if you dare to face our powerful ruler, follow me."

"We dare anything," said the Wizard, "so go ahead."

Through several marble corridors having lofty ceilings they passed, finding each corridor and doorway guarded by servants; but these servants of the palace were of the people and not giants, and they were so thin that they almost resembled skeletons. Finally they entered a great circular room with a high domed ceiling where the Czarover sat on a throne cut from a solid block of white marble and decorated with purple silk hangings and gold tassels.

The ruler of these people was combing his eyebrows when our friends entered his throne-room and stood before him, but he put the comb in his pocket and examined the strangers with evident curiosity. Then he said:

"Dear me, what a surprise! You have really

shocked me. For no outsider has ever before come to our City of Herku, and I cannot imagine why *you* have ventured to do so."

"We are looking for Ozma, the Supreme Ruler of the Land of Oz," replied the Wizard.

"Do you see her anywhere around here?" asked the Czarover.

"Not yet, Your Majesty; but perhaps you may tell us where she is."

"No; I have my hands full keeping track of my own people. I find them hard to manage because they are so tremendously strong."

"They don't look very strong," said Dorothy. "It seems as if a good wind would blow 'em way out of the city, if it wasn't for the wall."

"Just so—just so," admitted the Czarover. "They really look that way, don't they? But you must never trust to appearances, which have a way of fooling one. Perhaps you noticed that I prevented you from meeting any of my people. I protected you with my giants while you were on the way from the gates to my palace, so that not a Herku got near you."

"Are your people so dangerous, then?" asked the Wizard.

"To strangers, yes; but only because they are so friendly. For, if they shake hands with you, they are likely to break your arms or crush your fingers to a jelly."

"Why?" asked Button-Bright.

"Because we are the strongest people in all the world."

"Pshaw!" exclaimed the boy, "that's bragging. You prob'ly don't know how strong other people are. Why, once I knew a man in Philadelphi' who could bend iron bars with just his hands!"

"But—mercy me!—it's no trick to bend iron bars," said His Majesty. "Tell me, could this man crush a block of stone with his bare hands?"

"No one could do that," declared the boy.

"If I had a block of stone I'd show you," said the Czarover, looking around the room. "Ah, here is my throne. The back is too high, anyhow, so I'll just break off a piece of that."

He rose to his feet and tottered in an uncertain way around the throne. Then he took hold of the back and broke off a piece of marble over a foot thick.

"This," said he, coming back to his seat, "is very solid marble and much harder than ordinary stone. Yet I can crumble it easily with my fingers —a proof that I am very strong."

Even as he spoke he began breaking off chunks of marble and crumbling them as one would a bit of earth. The Wizard was so astonished that he took a piece in his own hands and tested it, finding it very hard indeed.

Just then one of the giant servants entered and exclaimed:

"Oh, Your Majesty, the cook has burned the soup! What shall we do?"

"How dare you interrupt me?" asked the Czarover, and grasping the immense giant by one of his legs he raised him in the air and threw him headfirst out of an open window.

"Now, tell me," he said, turning to Button-Bright, "could your man in Philadelphia crumble marble in his fingers?"

"I guess not," said Button-Bright, much impressed by the skinny monarch's strength.

"What makes you so strong?" inquired Dorothy.

"It's the zosozo," he explained, "which is an invention of my own. I and all my people eat zosozo, and it gives us tremendous strength. Would you like to eat some?"

"No, thank you," replied the girl. "I—I don't want to get so thin."

"Well, of course one can't have strength and flesh at the same time," said the Czarover. "Zosozo is pure energy, and it's the only compound of its sort in existence. I never allow our giants to have it, you know, or they would soon become our masters, since they are bigger than we; so I keep all the stuff locked up in my private laboratory. Once a year I feed a teaspoonful of it to each of my people—men, women and children—so every one of them is nearly as strong as I am. Wouldn't *you* like a dose, sir?"

he asked, turning to the Wizard.

"Well," said the Wizard, "if you would give me a little zosozo in a bottle, I'd like to take it with me on my travels. It might come handy, on occasion."

"To be sure. I'll give you enough for six doses," promised the Czarover. "But don't take more than a teaspoonful at a time. Once Ugu the Shoemaker took two teaspoonsful, and it made him so strong that when he leaned against the city wall he pushed it over, and we had to build it up again."

"Who is Ugu the Shoemaker?" asked Button-Bright curiously, for he now remembered that the bird and the rabbit had claimed Ugu the Shoemaker had enchanted the peach he had eaten.

"Why, Ugu is a great magician, who used to live here. But he's gone away, now," replied the Czarover.

"Where has he gone?" asked the Wizard quickly.

"I am told he lives in a wickerwork castle in the mountains to the west of here. You see, Ugu became such a powerful magician that he didn't care to live in our city any longer, for fear we would discover some of his secrets. So he went to the mountains and built him a splendid wicker castle, which is so strong that even I and my people could not batter it down, and there he lives all by himself."

"This is good news," declared the Wizard, "for I think this is just the magician we are searching for. But why is he called Ugu the Shoemaker?"

"Once he was a very common citizen here and made shoes for a living," replied the monarch of Herku. "But he was descended from the greatest wizard and sorcerer who has ever lived —in this or in any other country—and one day Ugu the Shoemaker discovered all the magical books and recipes of his famous great-grandfather, which had been hidden away in the attic of his house. So he began to study the papers and books and to practice magic, and in time he became so skillful that, as I said, he scorned our city and built a solitary castle for himself."

"Do you think," asked Dorothy anxiously, "that Ugu the Shoemaker would be wicked enough to steal our Ozma of Oz?"

"And the Magic Picture?" asked Trot.

"And the Great Book of Records of Glinda the Good?" asked Betsy.

"And my own magic tools?" asked the Wizard.

"Well," replied Czarover, "I won't say that Ugu is wicked, exactly, but he is very ambitious to become the most powerful magician in the world, and so I suppose he would not be too proud to steal any magic things that belonged to anybody else—if he could manage to do so."

"But how about Ozma? Why would he wish to steal *her?*" questioned Dorothy.

"Don't ask me, my dear. Ugu doesn't tell me why he does things, I assure you."

"Then we must go and ask him ourselves," declared the little girl.

"I wouldn't do that, if I were you," advised the Czarover, looking first at the three girls and then at the boy and the little Wizard and finally at the stuffed Patchwork Girl. "If Ugu has really stolen your Ozma, he will probably keep her a prisoner, in spite of all your threats or entreaties. And, with all his magical knowledge, he would be a dangerous person to attack. Therefore, if you are wise, you will go home again and find a new Ruler for the Emerald City and the Land of Oz. But perhaps it isn't Ugu the Shoemaker who has stolen your Ozma."

"The only way to settle that question," replied the Wizard, "is to go to Ugu's castle and see if Ozma is there. If she is, we will report the matter to the great Sorceress, Glinda the Good, and I'm pretty sure she will find a way to rescue our darling ruler from the Shoemaker."

"Well, do as you please," said the Czarover. "But, if you are all transformed into hummingbirds or caterpillars, don't blame me for not warning you."

They stayed the rest of that day in the City of

Herku and were fed at the royal table of the Czarover and given sleeping rooms in his palace. The strong monarch treated them very nicely and gave the Wizard a little golden vial of zosozo, to use if ever he or any of his party wished to acquire great strength.

Even at the last the Czarover tried to persuade them not to go near Ugu the Shoemaker, but they were resolved on the venture and the next morning bade the friendly monarch a cordial good-bye and, mounting upon their animals, left the Herkus and the City of Herku and headed for the mountains that lay to the west.

The Truth Pond

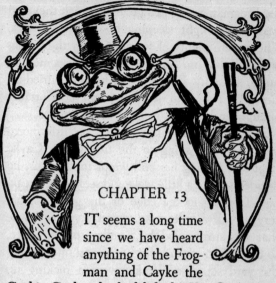

CHAPTER 13

IT seems a long time since we have heard anything of the Frog-man and Cayke the Cookie Cook, who had left the Yip Country in search of the diamond-studded gold dishpan which had been mysteriously stolen the same night that Ozma had disappeared from the Emerald City. But you must remember that while the Frogman and the Cookie Cook were preparing to descend from their mountain-top, and even while on their way to the farmhouse of Wiljon the Winkie, Dorothy and the Wizard and their friends were encountering the adventures we have just related.

So it was that on the very morning when the travelers from the Emerald City bade farewell to the Czarover of the City of Herku, Cayke and the Frogman awoke in a grove in which they had passed the night sleeping on beds of leaves. There were plenty of farmhouses in the neighborhood, but no one seemed to welcome the puffy, haughty Frogman or the little dried-up Cookie Cook, and so they slept comfortably enough underneath the trees of the grove.

The Frogman wakened first, on this morning, and after going to the tree where Cayke slept and finding her still wrapt in slumber, he decided to take a little walk and seek some breakfast. Coming to the edge of the grove he observed, half a mile away, a pretty yellow house that was surrounded by a yellow picket fence, so he walked toward this house and on entering the yard found a Winkie woman picking up sticks with which to build a fire to cook her morning meal.

"For goodness sakes!" she exclaimed on seeing the Frogman, "what are you doing out of your frogpond?"

"I am traveling in search of a jeweled gold dishpan, my good woman," he replied, with an air of great dignity.

"You won't find it here, then," said she. "Our dishpans are tin, and they're good enough for anybody. So go back to your pond and leave me alone."

She spoke rather crossly and with a lack of

respect that greatly annoyed the Frogman.

"Allow me to tell you, madam," he said, "that although I am a frog I am the Greatest and Wisest Frog in all the world. I may add that I possess much more wisdom than any Winkie— man or woman—in this land. Wherever I go, people fall on their knees before me and render homage to the Great Frogman! No one else knows so much as I; no one else is so grand— so magnificent!"

"If you know so much," she retorted, "why don't you know where your dishpan is, instead of chasing around the country after it?"

"Presently," he answered, "I am going where it is; but just now I am traveling and have had no breakfast. Therefore I honor you by asking you for something to eat."

"Oho! the Great Frogman is hungry as any tramp, is he? Then pick up these sticks and help me to build the fire," said the woman con- temptuously.

"Me! The Great Frogman pick up sticks?" he exclaimed in horror. "In the Yip Country, where I am more honored and powerful than any King could be, people weep with joy when I ask them to feed me."

"Then that's the place to go for your break- fast," declared the woman.

"I fear you do not realize my importance," urged the Frogman. "Exceeding wisdom renders me superior to menial duties."

"It's a great wonder to me," remarked the woman, carrying her sticks to the house, "that your wisdom doesn't inform you that you'll get no breakfast here," and she went in and slammed the door behind her.

The Frogman felt he had been insulted, so he gave a loud croak of indignation and turned away. After going a short distance he came upon a faint path which led across a meadow in the direction of a grove of pretty trees, and thinking this circle of evergreens must surround a house— where perhaps he would be kindly received—he decided to follow the path. And by and by he came to the trees, which were set close together, and pushing aside some branches he found no house inside the circle, but instead a very beautiful pond of clear water.

Now the Frogman, although he was so big and so well educated and now aped the ways and customs of human beings, was still a frog. As he gazed at this solitary, deserted pond, his love for water returned to him with irresistible force.

"If I cannot get a breakfast I may at least have a fine swim," said he, and pushing his way between the trees he reached the bank. There he took off his fine clothing, laying his shiny purple hat and his gold-headed cane beside it. A moment later he sprang with one leap into the water and dived to the very bottom of the pond.

The water was deliciously cool and grateful to his thick, rough skin, and the Frogman swam around the pond several times before he stopped to rest. Then he floated upon the surface and examined the pond with some curiosity. The bottom and sides were all lined with glossy tiles of a light pink color; just one place in the bottom, where the water bubbled up from a hidden spring, had been left free. On the banks the green grass grew to the edge of the pink tiling.

And now, as the Frogman examined the place, he found that on one side the pool, just above the water line, had been set a golden plate on which some words were deeply engraved. He swam toward this plate and on reaching it read the following inscription:

This is
THE TRUTH POND
*Whoever bathes in this
water must always
afterward tell*
THE TRUTH

This statement startled the Frogman. It even worried him, so that he leaped upon the bank and hurriedly began to dress himself.

"A great misfortune has befallen me," he told

THIS IS
THE TRUTH POND
Whoever bathes in this water
must be sure to tell
THE TRUTH

himself, "for hereafter I cannot tell people I am wise, since it is not the truth. The truth is that my boasted wisdom is all a sham, assumed by me to deceive people and make them defer to me. In truth, no living creature can know much more than his fellows, for one may know one thing, and another know another thing, so that wisdom is evenly scattered throughout the world. But—ah, me!—what a terrible fate will now be mine. Even Cayke the Cookie Cook will soon discover that my knowledge is no greater than her own; for having bathed in the enchanted water of the Truth Pond, I can no longer deceive her or tell a lie."

More humbled than he had been for many years, the Frogman went back to the grove where he had left Cayke and found the woman now awake and washing her face in a tiny brook.

"Where has Your Honor been?" she asked.

"To a farmhouse to ask for something to eat," said he, "but the woman refused me."

"How dreadful!" she exclaimed. "But never mind; there are other houses, where the people will be glad to feed the Wisest Creature in all the World."

"Do you mean yourself?" he asked.

"No, I mean you."

The Frogman felt strongly impelled to tell the truth, but struggled hard against it. His reason told him there was no use in letting Cayke know he was not wise, for then she would lose much respect for him, but each time he opened his mouth to speak he realized he was about to tell the truth and shut it again as quickly as possible. He tried to talk about something else, but the words necessary to undeceive the woman would force themselves to his lips in spite of all his struggles. Finally, knowing that he must either remain dumb or let the truth prevail, he gave a low groan of despair and said:

"Cayke, I am *not* the Wisest Creature in all the World; I am not wise at all."

"Oh, you must be!" she protested. "You told me so yourself, only last evening."

"Then last evening I failed to tell you the truth," he admitted, looking very shamefaced, for a frog. "I am sorry I told you that lie, my good Cayke; but, if you must know the truth, the whole truth and nothing but the truth, I am not really as wise as you are."

The Cookie Cook was greatly shocked to hear this, for it shattered one of her most pleasing illusions. She looked at the gorgeously dressed Frogman in amazement.

"What has caused you to change your mind so suddenly?" she inquired.

"I have bathed in the Truth Pond," he said, "and whoever bathes in that water is ever afterward obliged to tell the truth."

"You were foolish to do that," declared the

woman. "It is often very embarrassing to tell
the truth. I'm glad *I* didn't bathe in that dread
ful water!"

The Frogman looked at his companion
thoughtfully.

"Cayke," said he, "I want you to go to the
Truth Pond and take a bath in its water. For
if we are to travel together and encounter un
known adventures, it would not be fair that
alone must always tell you the truth, while you
could tell me whatever you pleased. If we both
dip in the enchanted water there will be n
chance in the future of our deceiving one an
other."

"No," she asserted, shaking her head pos
tively, "I won't do it, Your Honor. For, if I tol
you the truth, I'm sure you wouldn't like me. N
Truth Pond for me. I'll be just as I am, an hones

woman who can say what she wants to without hurting anyone's feelings."

With this decision the Frogman was forced to be content, although he was sorry the Cookie Cook would not listen to his advice.

The Unhappy Ferryman

CHAPTER 14

LEAVING the grove
where they had slept,
the Frogman and the
Cookie Cook turned
to the east to seek another house and after a short
walk came to one where the people received
them very politely. The children stared rather
hard at the big, pompous Frogman, but the
woman of the house, when Cayke asked for
something to eat, at once brought them food
and said they were welcome to it.

"Few people in need of help pass this way,"
she remarked, "for the Winkies are all prosper-
ous and love to stay in their own homes. But
perhaps you are not a Winkie," she added.

"No," said Cayke, "I am a Yip, and my home

is on a high mountain at the southeast of your country."

"And the Frogman—is he, also, a Yip?"

"I do not know what he is, other than a very remarkable and highly educated creature," replied the Cookie Cook. "But he has lived many years among the Yips, who have found him so wise and intelligent that they always go to him for advice."

"May I ask why you have left your home, and where you are going?" said the Winkie woman.

Then Cayke told her of the diamond-studded gold dishpan and how it had been mysteriously stolen from her house, after which she had discovered that she could no longer cook good cookies. So she had resolved to search until she found her dishpan again, because a Cookie Cook who cannot cook good cookies is not of much use. The Frogman, who wanted to see more of the world, had accompanied her to assist in the search. When the woman had listened to this story she asked.

"Then you have no idea, as yet, who has stolen your dishpan?"

"I only know it must have been some mischievous fairy, or a magician, or some such powerful person, because none other could have climbed the steep mountain to the Yip Country. And who else could have carried away my

beautiful, magic dishpan without being seen?"

The woman thought about this during the time that Cayke and the Frogman ate their breakfast. When they had finished she said:

"Where are you going next?"

"We have not decided," answered the Cookie Cook.

"Our plan," explained the Frogman, in his important way, "is to travel from place to place until we learn where the thief is located, and then to force him to return the dishpan to its proper owner."

"The plan is all right," agreed the woman, "but it may take you a long time before you succeed, your method being sort of haphazard and indefinite. However, I advise you to travel toward the east."

"Why?" asked the Frogman.

"Because if you went west you would soon come to the desert, and also because in this part of the Winkie Country no one steals, so your time here would be wasted. But toward the east, beyond the river, live many strange people whose honesty I would not vouch for. Moreover, if you journey far enough east and cross the river for a second time, you will come to the Emerald City, where there is much magic and sorcery. The Emerald City is ruled by a dear little girl called Ozma, who also rules the Emperor of the Winkies and all the Land of Oz. So, as Ozma is a fairy, she may be able to tell you just who has taken your precious dishpan. Provided, of course, you do not find it before you reach her."

"This seems to me to be excellent advice," said the Frogman, and Cayke agreed with him.

"The most sensible thing for you to do," continued the woman, "would be to return to your home and use another dishpan, learning to cook cookies as other people cook cookies, without the aid of magic. But, if you cannot be happy without the magic dishpan you have lost, you are likely to learn more about it in the Emerald City than at any other place in Oz."

They thanked the good woman and on leaving her house faced the east and continued in that direction all the way. Toward evening they came to the west branch of the Winkie River and there, on the river bank, found a ferryman who lived all alone in a little yellow house.

This ferryman was a Winkie with a very small head and a very large body. He was sitting in his doorway as the travelers approached him and did not even turn his head to look at them.

"Good evening," said the Frogman.

The ferryman made no reply.

"We would like some supper and the privilege of sleeping in your house until morning," continued the Frogman. "At daybreak we would like some breakfast and then we would like to have you row us across the river."

The ferryman neither moved nor spoke. He sat in his doorway and looked straight ahead.

"I think he must be deaf and dumb," Cayke whispered to her companion. Then she stood directly in front of the ferryman and putting her mouth close to his ear she yelled as loudly as she could:

"Good evening!"

The ferryman scowled.

"Why do you yell at me, woman?" he asked.

"Can you hear what I say?" she asked in her ordinary tone of voice.

"Of course," replied the man.

"Then why didn't you answer the Frogman?"

"Because," said the ferryman, "I don't understand the frog language."

"He speaks the same words that I do and in the same way," declared Cayke.

"Perhaps," replied the ferryman; "but to me his voice sounded like a frog's croak. I know that in the Land of Oz animals can speak our language, and so can the birds and bugs and fishes; but in *my* ears they sound merely like growls and chirps and croaks."

"Why is that?" asked the Cookie Cook in surprise.

"Once, many years ago, I cut the tail off a fox which had taunted me; and I stole some birds' eggs from a nest to make an omelet with, and also I pulled a fish from the river and left it lying on the bank to gasp for lack of water until it died. I don't know why I did those wicked things, but I did them. So the Emperor of the Winkies—who is the Tin Woodman and has a very tender tin heart—punished me by denying me any communication with beasts, birds or fishes. I cannot understand them when they speak to me, although I know that other people can do so, nor can the creatures understand a word I say to them. Every time I meet one of them I am reminded of my former cruelty, and it makes me very unhappy."

"Really," said Cayke, "I'm sorry for you, although the Tin Woodman is not to blame for punishing you."

"What is he mumbling about?" asked the Frogman.

"He is talking to me, but you don't understand him," she replied. And then she told him of the ferryman's punishment and afterward explained to the ferryman that they wanted to stay all night with him and be fed.

He gave them some fruit and bread, which was the only sort of food he had, and he allowed Cayke to sleep in a room of his cottage. But the Frogman he refused to admit to his house, saying that the frog's presence made him miserable and unhappy. At no time would he look directly at the Frogman, or even toward him, fearing he

would shed tears if he did so; so the big frog slept on the river bank, where he could hear little frogs croaking in the river all the night through. But that did not keep him awake; it merely soothed him to slumber, for he realized how much superior he was to them.

Just as the sun was rising on a new day the ferryman rowed the two travelers across the river —keeping his back to the Frogman all the way —and then Cayke thanked him and bade him good-bye and the ferryman rowed home again.

On this side the river there were no paths at all, so it was evident they had reached a part of the country little frequented by travelers. There was a marsh at the south of them, sand-hills at the north and a growth of scrubby underbrush leading toward a forest at the east. So the east was really the least difficult way to go and that direction was the one they had determined to follow.

Now the Frogman, although he wore green patent-leather shoes with ruby buttons, had very large and flat feet, and when he tramped through the scrub his weight crushed down the underbrush and made a path for Cayke to follow him. Therefore they soon reached the forest, where the tall trees were set far apart but were so leafy that they shaded all the spaces between them with their branches.

The Unhappy Ferryman

"There are no bushes here," said Cayke, much pleased, "so we can now travel faster and with more comfort."

The Big Lavender Bear

CHAPTER 15

IT was a pleasant
place to wander in
and the two travelers
were proceeding at a
brisk pace when suddenly a voice shouted:
"Halt!"

They looked around in surprise, seeing at
first no one at all. Then from behind a tree
there stepped a brown fuzzy bear, whose head
came about as high as Cayke's waist—and Cayke
was a small woman. The bear was chubby as well
as fuzzy; his body was even puffy, while his legs
and arms seemed jointed at the knees and elbows
and fastened to his body by pins or rivets. His
ears were round in shape and stuck out in a
comical way, while his round black eyes were
bright and sparkling as beads. Over his shoulder

the little brown bear bore a gun with a tin barrel. The barrel had a cork in the end of it and a string was attached to the cork and to the handle of the gun.

Both the Frogman and Cayke gazed hard at this curious bear, standing silent for some time. But finally the Frogman recovered from his surprise and remarked:

"It seems to me that you are stuffed with sawdust and ought not to be alive."

"That's all you know about it," answered the little Brown Bear in a squeaky voice. "I am stuffed with a very good quality of curled hair and my skin is the best plush that was ever made. As for my being alive, that is my own affair and cannot concern you at all—except that it gives me the privilege to say you are my prisoners."

"Prisoners! Why do you speak such nonsense?" asked the Frogman angrily. "Do you think we are afraid of a toy bear with a toy gun?"

"You ought to be," was the confident reply, "for I am merely the sentry guarding the way to Bear Center, which is a city containing hundreds of my race, who are ruled by a very powerful sorcerer known as the Lavender Bear. He ought to be a purple color, you know, seeing he is a King, but he's only light lavender, which is, of course, second-cousin to royal purple. So, unless you come with me peaceably, as my prisoners, I shall fire my gun and bring a hundred bears—of all sizes and colors—to capture you."

"Why do you wish to capture us?" inquired the Frogman, who had listened to this speech with much astonishment.

"I don't wish to, as a matter of fact," replied the little Brown Bear, "but it is my duty to, because you are now trespassing on the domain of His Majesty the King of Bear Center. Also I will admit that things are rather quiet in our city, just now, and the excitement of your capture, followed by your trial and execution, should afford us much entertainment."

"We defy you!" said the Frogman.

"Oh, no; don't do that," pleaded Cayke, speaking to her companion. "He says his King is a sorcerer, so perhaps it is he or one of his bears who ventured to steal my jeweled dishpan. Let us go to the City of the Bears and discover if my dishpan is there."

"I must now register one more charge against you," remarked the little Brown Bear, with evident satisfaction. "You have just accused us of stealing, and that is such a dreadful thing to say that I am quite sure our noble King will command you to be executed."

"But how could you execute us?" inquired the Cookie Cook.

"I've no idea. But our King is a wonderful inventor and there is no doubt he can find a proper way to destroy you. So, tell me, are you going to struggle, or will you go peaceably to meet your doom?"

It was all so ridiculous that Cayke laughed aloud and even the Frogman's wide mouth curled in a smile. Neither was a bit afraid to go to the Bear City and it seemed to both that there was a possibility they might discover the missing dishpan. So the Frogman said:

"Lead the way, little Bear, and we will follow without a struggle."

"That's very sensible of you; very sensible, indeed!" declared the Brown Bear. "So—forward *march!*" and with the command he turned around and began to waddle along a path that led between the trees.

Cayke and the Frogman, as they followed their conductor, could scarce forbear laughing at his stiff, awkward manner of walking and, although he moved his stuffy legs fast, his steps were so short that they had to go slowly in order not to run into him. But after a time they reached a large, circular space in the center of the forest, which was clear of any stumps or underbrush. The ground was covered by a soft gray moss, pleasant to tread upon. All the trees surrounding this space seemed to be hollow and had round holes in their trunks, set a little way above

the ground, but otherwise there was nothing
unusual about the place and nothing in the opin
ion of the prisoners, to indicate a settlement
But the little Brown Bear said in a proud and
impressive voice (although it still squeaked)

"This is the wonderful city known to fame
as Bear Center!"

"But there are no houses; there are no bear
living here at all!" exclaimed Cayke.

"Oh, indeed!" retorted their captor and rais
ing his gun he pulled the trigger. The cork flew
out of the tin barrel with a loud "pop!" and a
once from every hole in ever tree within view
of the clearing appeared the head of a bear
They were of many colors and of many sizes, bu
all were made in the same manner as the bear
who had met and captured them.

At first a chorus of growls arose and then
sharp voice cried:

"What has happened, Corporal Waddle?"

"Captives, Your Majesty!" answered th
Brown Bear. "Intruders upon our domain an
slanderers of our good name."

"Ah, that's important," answered the voice

Then from out the hollow trees tumbled
whole regiment of stuffed bears, some carryin
tin swords, some popguns and other long spear
with gay ribbons tied to the handles. Ther
were hundreds of them, altogether, and the
quickly formed a circle around the Frogman an

the Cookie Cook but kept at a distance and left a large space for the prisoners to stand in.

Presently this circle parted and into the center of it stalked a huge toy bear of a lovely lavender color. He walked upon his hind legs, as did all the others, and on his head he wore a tin crown set with diamonds and amethysts, while in one paw he carried a short wand of some glittering metal that resembled silver but wasn't.

"His Majesty the King!" shouted Corporal Waddle, and all the bears bowed low. Some bowed so low that they lost their balance and toppled over, but they soon scrambled up again and the Lavender King squatted on his haunches before the prisoners and gazed at them steadily with his bright pink eyes.

The Little Pink Bear

CHAPTER 16

"ONE Person and one Freak," said the big Lavender Bear, when he had carefully examined the strangers.

"I am sorry to hear you call poor Cayke the Cookie Cook a Freak," remonstrated the Frogman.

"She is the Person," asserted the King. "Unless I am mistaken, it is you who are the Freak."

The Frogman was silent, for he could not truthfully deny it.

"Why have you dared intrude in my forest?" demanded the Bear King.

"We didn't know it *was* your forest," said Cayke, "and we are on our way to the far east, where the Emerald City is."

"Ah, it's a long way from here to the Emerald City," remarked the King. "It is so far away, indeed, that no bear among us has ever been there. But what errand requires you to travel such a distance?"

"Someone has stolen my diamond-studded gold dishpan," explained Cayke; "and, as I cannot be happy without it, I have decided to search the world over until I find it again. The Frogman, who is very learned and wonderfully wise, has come with me to give me his assistance. Isn't it kind of him?"

The King looked at the Frogman.

"What makes you so wonderfully wise?" he asked.

"I'm not," was the candid reply. "The Cookie Cook, and some others in the Yip Country, think because I am a big frog and talk and act like a man, that I must be very wise. I have learned more than a frog usually knows, it is true, but I am not yet so wise as I hope to become at some future time."

The King nodded, and when he did so something squeaked in his chest.

"Did Your Majesty speak?" asked Cayke.

"Not just then," answered the Lavender Bear, seeming to be somewhat embarrassed. "I am so built, you must know, that when anything pushes against my chest, as my chin accidentally did just then, I make that silly noise. In this city it isn't considered good manners to notice it. But I like your Frogman. He is honest and truthful, which is more than can be said of many others. As for your late lamented dishpan, I'll show it to you."

With this he waved three times the metal wand which he held in his paw and instantly there appeared upon the ground, midway between the King and Cayke, a big round pan made of beaten gold. Around the top edge was a row of small diamonds; around the center of the pan was another row of larger diamonds; and at the bottom was a row of exceedingly large and brilliant diamonds. In fact, they all sparkled magnificently and the pan was so big and broad that it took a lot of diamonds to go around it three times.

Cayke stared so hard that her eyes seemed about to pop out of her head.

"O-o-o-oh!" she exclaimed, drawing a deep breath of delight.

"Is this your dishpan?" inquired the King.

"It is—it is!" cried the Cookie Cook, and rushing forward she fell on her knees and threw her arms around the precious pan. But her arms came together without meeting any resistance at all. Cayke tried to seize the edge, but found nothing to grasp. The pan was surely there, she thought, for she could see it plainly; but it was not solid; she could not feel it at all. With a

moan of astonishment and despair she raised her
head to look at the Bear King, who was watching
her actions curiously. Then she turned to the
pan again, only to find it had completely disappeared.

"Poor creature!" murmured the King pity-
ingly. "You must have thought, for the moment,
that you had actually recovered your dishpan.
But what you saw was merely the image of it,
conjured up by means of my magic. It is a pretty
dishpan, indeed, though rather big and awkward
to handle. I hope you will some day find it."

Cayke was grievously disappointed. She began
to cry, wiping her eyes on her apron. The King
turned to the throng of toy bears surrounding
him and asked:

"Has any of you ever seen this golden dishpan before?"

"No," they answered in a chorus.

The King seemed to reflect. Presently he inquired:

"Where is the Little Pink Bear?"

"At home, Your Majesty," was the reply.

"Fetch him here," commanded the King.

Several of the bears waddled over to one of
the trees and pulled from its hollow a tiny pink
bear, smaller than any of the others. A big
white bear carried the pink one in his arms and
set it down beside the King, arranging the joints
of its legs so that it would stand upright.

This Pink Bear seemed lifeless until the King turned a crank which protruded from its side, when the little creature turned its head stiffly from side to side and said in a small shrill voice:

"Hurrah for the King of Bear Center!"

"Very good," said the big Lavender Bear; "he seems to be working very well to-day. Tell me, my Pink Pinkerton, what has become of this lady's jeweled dishpan?"

"U—u—u," said the Pink Bear, and then stopped short.

The King turned the crank again.

"U-g-u the Shoemaker has it," said the Pink Bear.

"Who is Ugu the Shoemaker?" demanded the King, again turning the crank.

"A magician who lives on a mountain in a wickerwork castle," was the reply.

"Where is this mountain?" was the next question.

"Nineteen miles and three furlongs from Bear Center to the northeast."

"And is the dishpan still at the castle of Ugu the Shoemaker?" asked the King.

"It is."

The King turned to Cayke.

"You may rely on this information," said he. "The Pink Bear can tell us anything we wish to know, and his words are always words of truth."

The Little Pink Bear

"Is he alive?" asked the Frogman, much interested in the Pink Bear.

"Something animates him—when you turn his crank," replied the King. "I do not know if it is life, or what it is, or how it happens that the Little Pink Bear can answer correctly every question put to him. We discovered his talent a long time ago and whenever we wish to know anything—which is not very often—we ask the Pink Bear. There is no doubt whatever, madam, that Ugu the Magician has your dishpan, and if you dare go to him you may be able to recover it. But of that I am not certain."

"Can't the Pink Bear tell?" asked Cayke anxiously.

"No, for that is in the future. He can tell anything that *has* happened, but nothing that is going to happen. Don't ask me why, for I don't know."

"Well," said the Cookie Cook, after a little thought, "I mean to go to this magician, anyhow, and tell him I want my dishpan. I wish I knew what Ugu the Shoemaker is like."

"Then I'll show him to you," promised the King. "But do not be frightened; it won't be Ugu, remember, but only his image."

With this he waved his metal wand again and in the circle suddenly appeared a thin little man, very old and skinny, who was seated on a wicker stool before a wicker table. On the table

lay a Great Book with gold clasps. The Book was open and the man was reading in it. He wore great spectacles, which were fastened before his eyes by means of a ribbon that passed around his head and was tied in a bow at the back. His hair was very thin and white; his skin, which clung fast to his bones, was brown and seared with furrows; he had a big, fat nose and little eyes set close together.

On no account was Ugu the Shoemaker a pleasant person to gaze at. As his image appeared before them, all were silent and intent until Corporal Waddle, the Brown Bear, became nervous and pulled the trigger of his gun. Instantly the cork flew out of the tin barrel with a loud "pop!" that made them all jump. And, at this sound, the image of the magician vanished.

"So! *that's* the thief, is it?" said Cayke, in an angry voice. "I should think he'd be ashamed of himself for stealing a poor woman's diamond dishpan! But I mean to face him in his wicker castle and force him to return my property."

"To me," said the Bear King, reflectively, "he looked like a dangerous person. I hope he won't be so unkind as to argue the matter with you."

The Frogman was much disturbed by the vision of Ugu the Shoemaker, and Cayke's determination to go to the magician filled her companion with misgivings. But he would not break his pledged word to assist the Cookie Cook and after breathing a deep sigh of resignation he asked the King:

"Will Your Majesty lend us this Pink Bear who answers questions, that we may take him with us on our journey? He would be very useful to us and we will promise to bring him safely back to you."

The King did not reply at once; he semed to be thinking.

"*Please* let us take the Pink Bear," begged Cayke. "I'm sure he would be a great help to us."

"The Pink Bear," said the King, "is the best bit of magic I possess, and there is not another like him in the world. I do not care to let him out of my sight; nor do I wish to disappoint you; so I believe I will make the journey in your company and carry my Pink Bear with me. He can walk, when you wind the other side of him, but so slowly and awkwardly that he would delay you. But if I go along I can carry him in my arms, so I will join your party. Whenever you are ready to start, let me know."

"But—Your Majesty!" exclaimed Corporal Waddle in protest, "I hope you do not intend to let these prisoners escape without punishment."

"Of what crime do you accuse them?" inquired the King.

"Why, they trespassed on your domain, for

one thing," said the Brown Bear.

"We didn't know it was private property, Your Majesty," said the Cookie Cook.

"And they asked if any of us had stolen the dishpan!" continued Corporal Waddle indignantly. "That is the same thing as calling us thieves and robbers, and bandits and brigands, is it not?"

"Every person has the right to ask questions," said the Frogman.

"But the Corporal is quite correct," declared the Lavender Bear. "I condemn you both to death, the execution to take place ten years from this hour."

"But we belong in the Land of Oz, where no one ever dies," Cayke reminded him.

"Very true," said the King. "I condemn you to death merely as a matter of form. It sounds quite terrible, and in ten years we shall have forgotten all about it. Are you ready to start for the wicker castle of Ugu the Shoemaker?"

"Quite ready, Your Majesty."

"But who will rule in your place, while you are gone?" asked a big Yellow Bear.

"I myself will rule while I am gone," was the reply. "A King isn't required to stay at home forever, and if he takes a notion to travel, whose business is it but his own? All I ask is that you bears behave yourselves while I am away. If any of you is naughty, I'll send him to some girl

or boy in America to play with."

This dreadful threat made all the toy bears look solemn. They assured the King, in a chorus of growls, that they would be good. Then the big Lavender Bear picked up the little Pink Bear and after tucking it carefully under one arm he said "Good-bye till I come back!" and waddled along the path that led through the forest. The Frogman and Cayke the Cookie Cook also said good-bye to the bears and then followed after the King, much to the regret of the little Brown Bear, who pulled the trigger of his gun and popped the cork as a parting salute.

The Meeting

CHAPTER 17

WHILE the Frog-
man and his party
were advancing from
the west, Dorothy
and her party were advancing from the east, and
so it happened that on the following night they
all camped at a little hill that was only a few
miles from the wicker castle of Ugu the Shoemaker. But the two parties did not see one
another that night, for one camped on one side of
the hill while the other camped on the opposite
side. But the next morning the Frogman thought
he would climb the hill and see what was on
top of it, and at the same time Scraps, the
Patchwork Girl, also decided to climb the hill
to find if the wicker castle was visible from its
top. So she stuck her head over an edge just as

the Frogman's head appeared over another edge and both, being surprised, kept still while they took a good look at one another.

Scraps recovered from her astonishment first and bounding upward she turned a somersault and landed sitting down and facing the big Frogman, who slowly advanced and sat opposite her.

"Well met, Stranger!" cried the Patchwork Girl, with a whoop of laughter. "You are quite the funniest individual I have seen in all my travels."

"Do you suppose I can be any funnier than you?" asked the Frogman, gazing at her in wonder.

"I'm not funny to myself, you know," returned Scraps. "I wish I were. And perhaps you are so used to your own absurd shape that you do not laugh whenever you see your reflection in a pool, or in a mirror."

"No," said the Frogman gravely, "I do not. I used to be proud of my great size and vain of my culture and education, but since I bathed in the Truth Pond I sometimes think it is not right that I should be different from all other frogs."

"Right or wrong," said the Patchwork Girl, "to be different is to be distinguished. Now, in my case, I'm just like all other Patchwork Girls because I'm the only one there is. But, tell me,

where did you come from?"

"The Yip Country," said he.

"Is that in the Land of Oz?"

"Of course," replied the Frogman.

"And do you know that your Ruler, Ozma of Oz, has been stolen?"

"I was not aware that I had a Ruler, so of course I couldn't know that she was stolen."

"Well, you have. All the people of Oz," explained Scraps, "are ruled by Ozma, whether they know it or not. And she has been stolen. Aren't you angry? Aren't you indignant? Your Ruler, whom you didn't know you had, has positively been stolen!"

"That is queer," remarked the Frogman thoughtfully. "Stealing is a thing practically unknown in Oz, yet this Ozma has been taken and a friend of mine has also had her dishpan stolen. With her I have traveled all the way from the Yip Country in order to recover it."

"I don't see any connection between a Royal Ruler of Oz and a dishpan!" declared Scraps.

"They've both been stolen, haven't they?"

"True. But why can't your friend wash her dishes in another dishpan?" asked Scraps.

"Why can't you use another Royal Ruler? I suppose you prefer the one who is lost, and my friend wants her own dishpan, which is made of gold and studded with diamonds and has magic powers."

"Magic, eh?" exclaimed Scraps. "*There* is a link that connects the two steals, anyhow, for it seems that all the magic in the Land of Oz was stolen at the same time, whether it was in the Emerald City or in Glinda's castle or in the Yip Country. Seems mighty strange and mysterious, doesn't it?"

"It used to seem that way to us," admitted the Frogman, "but we have now discovered who took our dishpan. It was Ugu the Shoemaker."

"Ugu? Good gracious! That's the same magician we think has stolen Ozma. We are now on our way to the castle of this Shoemaker."

"So are we," said the Frogman.

"Then follow me, quick! and let me introduce you to Dorothy and the other girls and to the Wizard of Oz and all the rest of us."

She sprang up and seized his coat-sleeve, dragging him off the hilltop and down the other side from that whence he had come. And at the foot of the hill the Frogman was astonished to find the three girls and the Wizard and Button-Bright, who were surrounded by a wooden Sawhorse, a lean Mule, a square Woozy and a Cowardly Lion. A little black dog ran up and smelled at the Frogman, but couldn't growl at him.

"I've discovered another party that has been robbed," shouted Scraps as she joined them. "This is their leader and they're all going to

Ugu's castle to fight the wicked Shoemaker!"

They regarded the Frogman with much curiosity and interest and, finding all eyes fixed upon him, the newcomer arranged his necktie and smoothed his beautiful vest and swung his gold-headed cane like a regular dandy. The big spectacles over his eyes quite altered his froglike countenance and gave him a learned and impressive look. Used as she was to seeing strange creatures in the Land of Oz, Dorothy was amazed at discovering the Frogman. So were all her companions. Toto wanted to growl at him, but couldn't, and he didn't dare bark. The Sawhorse snorted rather contemptuously, but the Lion whispered to the wooden steed: "Bear with this strange creature, my friend, and remember he is no more extraordinary than you are. Indeed, it is more natural for a frog to be big than for a Sawhorse to be alive."

On being questioned, the Frogman told them the whole story of the loss of Cayke's highly prized dishpan and their adventures in search of it. When he came to tell of the Lavender Bear King and of the Little Pink Bear who could tell anything you wanted to know, his hearers became eager to see such interesting animals.

"It will be best," said the Wizard, "to unite our two parties and share our fortunes together, for we are all bound on the same errand and as one band we may more easily defy this shoemaker magician than if separate. Let us be allies."

"I will ask my friends about that," replied the Frogman, and climbed over the hill to find Cayke and the toy bears. The Patchwork Girl accompanied him and when they came upon the Cookie Cook and the Lavender Bear and the Pink Bear it was hard to tell which of the lot was the most surprised.

"Mercy me!" cried Cayke, addressing the Patchwork Girl. "However did you come alive?"

Scraps stared at the bears.

"Mercy me!" she echoed; "you are stuffed, as I am, with cotton, and yet you appear to be living. That makes me feel ashamed, for I have prided myself on being the only live cotton-stuffed person in Oz."

"Perhaps you are," returned the Lavender Bear, "for I am stuffed with extra-quality curled hair, and so is the Little Pink Bear."

"You have relieved my mind of a great anxiety," declared the Patchwork Girl, now speaking more cheerfully. "The Scarecrow is stuffed with straw, and you with hair, so I am still the Original and Only Cotton-Stuffed!"

"I hope I am too polite to criticize cotton, as compared with curled hair," said the King, "especially as you seem satisfied with it."

Then the Frogman told of his interview with

the party from the Emerald City and added that
the Wizard of Oz had invited the bears and
Cayke and himself to travel in company with
them to the castle of Ugu the Shoemaker. Cayke
was much pleased, but the Bear King looked
solemn. He set the Little Pink Bear on his lap
and turned the crank in its side and asked:

"Is it safe for us to associate with those people
from the Emerald City?"

And the Pink Bear at once replied:

"Safe for you and safe for me;
Perhaps no others safe will be."

"That 'perhaps' need not worry us," said the
King; "so let us join the others and offer them
our protection."

Even the Lavender Bear was astonished, however, when on climbing over the hill he found
on the other side the group of queer animals and
the people from the Emerald City. The bears
and Cayke were received very cordially, although Button-Bright was cross when they
wouldn't let him play with the Little Pink Bear.
The three girls greatly admired the toy bears,
and especially the pink one, which they longed
to hold.

"You see," explained the Lavender King, in
denying them this privilege, "he's a very valuable
bear, because his magic is a correct guide on all
occasions, and especially if one is in difficulties.

It was the Pink Bear who told us that Ugu the Shoemaker had stolen the Cookie Cook's dishpan."

"And the King's magic is just as wonderful," added Cayke, "because it showed us the Magician himself."

"What did he look like?" inquired Dorothy.

"He was dreadful!"

"He was sitting at a table and examining an immense Book which had three golden clasps," remarked the King.

"Why, that must have been Glinda's Great Book of Records!" exclaimed Dorothy. "If it is, it proves that Ugu the Shoemaker stole Ozma, and with her all the magic in the Emerald City."

"And my dishpan," said Cayke. And the Wizard added:

"It also proves that he is following our adventures in the Book of Records, and therefore knows that we are seeking him and that we are determined to find him and rescue Ozma at all hazards."

"If we can," added the Woozy, but everybody frowned at him.

The Wizard's statement was so true that the faces around him were very serious until the Patchwork Girl broke into a peal of laughter.

"Wouldn't it be a rich joke if he made prisoners of *us*, too?" she said.

"No one but a crazy Patchwork Girl would

consider *that* a joke," grumbled Button-Bright. And then the Lavender Bear King asked:

"Would you like to see this magical shoe-maker?"

"Wouldn't he know it?" Dorothy inquired.

"No, I think not."

Then the King waved his metal wand and before them appeared a room in the wicker castle of Ugu. On the wall of the room hung Ozma's Magic Picture, and seated before it was the Magician. They could see the Picture as well as he could, because it faced them, and in the Picture was the hillside where they were now sitting, all their forms being reproduced in miniature. And, curiously enough, within the scene of the Picture was the scene they were now beholding, so they knew that the Magician was at this moment watching them in the Picture, and also that he saw himself and the room he was in become visible to the people on the hillside. Therefore he knew very well that they were watching him while he was watching them.

In proof of this, Ugu sprang from his seat and turned a scowling face in their direction; but now he could not see the travelers who were seeking him, although they could still see him. His actions were so distinct, indeed, that it seemed he was actually before them.

"It is only a ghost," said the Bear King. "It

isn't real at all, except that it shows us Ugu just as he looks and tells us truly just what he is doing."

"I don't see anything of my lost growl, though," said Toto, as if to himself.

Then the vision faded away and they could see nothing but the grass and trees and bushes around them.

The Conference

"NOW, THEN,"

CHAPTER 18

"NOW, then," said the Wizard, "let us talk this matter over and decide what to do when we get to Ugu's wicker castle. There can be no doubt that the Shoemaker is a powerful Magician, and his powers have been increased a hundredfold since he secured the Great Book of Records, the Magic Picture, all of Glinda's recipes for sorcery and my own black bag—which was full of tools of wizardry. The man who could rob us of those things, and the man with all their powers at his command, is one who may prove somewhat difficult to conquer; therefore we should plan our actions well before we venture too near to his castle."

"I didn't see Ozma in the Magic Picture,"

said Trot. "What do you suppose Ugu has done with her?"

"Couldn't the Little Pink Bear tell us what he did with Ozma?" asked Button-Bright.

"To be sure," replied the Lavender King; "I'll ask him."

So he turned the crank in the Little Pink Bear's side and inquired:

"Did Ugu the Shoemaker steal Ozma of Oz?"

"Yes," answered the Little Pink Bear.

"Then what did he do with her?" asked the King.

"Shut her up in a dark place," answered the Little Pink Bear.

"Oh, that must be a dungeon cell!" cried Dorothy, horrified. "How dreadful!"

"Well, we must get her out of it," said the Wizard. "That is what we came for and of course we must rescue Ozma. But—how?"

Each one looked at some other one for an answer and all shook their heads in a grave and dismal manner. All but Scraps, who danced around them gleefully.

"You're afraid," said the Patchwork Girl, "because so many things can hurt your meat bodies. Why don't you give it up and go home? How can you fight a great magician when you have nothing to fight with?"

Dorothy looked at her reflectively.

"Scraps," said she, "you know that Ugu

couldn't hurt you, a bit, whatever he did; nor could he hurt *me*, 'cause I wear the Nome King's Magic Belt. S'pose just we two go on together, and leave the others here to wait for us?"

"No, no!" said the Wizard positively. "That won't do at all. Ozma is more powerful than either of you, yet she could not defeat the wicked Ugu, who has shut her up in a dungeon. We must go to the Shoemaker in one mighty band, for only in union is there strength."

"That is excellent advice," said the Lavender Bear, approvingly.

"But what can we do, when we get to Ugu?" inquired the Cookie Cook anxiously.

"Do not expect a prompt answer to that important question," replied the Wizard, "for we must first plan our line of conduct. Ugu knows, of course, that we are after him, for he has seen our approach in the Magic Picture, and he has read of all we have done up to the present moment in the Great Book of Records. Therefore we cannot expect to take him by surprise."

"Don't you suppose Ugu would listen to reason?" asked Betsy. "If we explained to him how wicked he has been, don't you think he'd let poor Ozma go?"

"And give me back my dishpan?" added the Cookie Cook eagerly.

"Yes, yes; won't he say he's sorry and get on his knees and beg our pardon?" cried Scraps, turning a flip-flop to show her scorn of the suggestion. "When Ugu the Shoemaker does that, please knock at the front door and let me know."

The Wizard sighed and rubbed his bald head with a puzzled air.

"I'm quite sure Ugu will not be polite to us," said he, "so we must conquer this cruel magician by force, much as we dislike to be rude to anyone. But none of you has yet suggested a way to do that. Couldn't the Little Pink Bear tell us how?" he asked, turning to the Bear King.

"No, for that is something that is *going* to happen," replied the Lavender Bear. "He can only tell us what already *has* happened."

Again they were grave and thoughtful. But after a time Betsy said in a hesitating voice:

"Hank is a great fighter; perhaps *he* could conquer the magician."

The Mule turned his head to look reproachfully at his old friend, the young girl.

"Who can fight against magic?" he asked.

"The Cowardly Lion could," said Dorothy.

The Lion, who was lying with his front legs spread out, his chin on his paws, raised his shaggy head.

"I can fight when I'm not afraid," said he calmly; "but the mere mention of a fight sets me to trembling."

"Ugu's magic couldn't hurt the Sawhorse," suggested tiny Trot.

"And the Sawhorse couldn't hurt the Magician," declared that wooden animal.

"For my part," said Toto, "I am helpless, having lost my growl."

"Then," said Cayke the Cookie Cook, "we must depend upon the Frogman. His marvelous wisdom will surely inform him how to conquer the wicked Magician and restore to me my dishpan."

All eyes were now turned questioningly upon the Frogman. Finding himself the center of observation, he swung his gold-headed cane, adjusted his big spectacles and after swelling out his chest, sighed and said in a modest tone of voice:

"Respect for truth obliges me to confess that Cayke is mistaken in regard to my superior wisdom. I am not very wise. Neither have I had any practical experience in conquering magicians. But let us consider this case. What is Ugu, and what is a magician? Ugu is a renegade shoemaker and a magician is an ordinary man who, having learned how to do magical tricks, considers himself above his fellows. In this case, the Shoemaker has been naughty enough to steal a lot of magical tools and things that did not belong to him, and it is more wicked to steal than to be a magician. Yet, with all the arts at his command, Ugu is still a man, and surely there are ways in which a man may be conquered. How, do you say, how? Allow me to state that I don't know. In my judgment we cannot decide how best to act until we get to Ugu's castle. So let us go to it and take a look at it. After that we may discover an idea that will guide us to victory."

"That may not be a wise speech, but it sounds good," said Dorothy approvingly. "Ugu the Shoemaker is not only a common man, but he's a wicked man and a cruel man and deserves to be conquered. We mustn't have any mercy on him till Ozma is set free. So let's go to his castle, as the Frogman says, and see what the place looks like."

No one offered an objection to this plan and so it was adopted. They broke camp and were about to start on the journey to Ugu's castle when they discovered that Button-Bright was lost again. The girls and the Wizard shouted his name and the Lion roared and the Donkey brayed and the Frogman croaked and the Big Lavender Bear growled (to the envy of Toto, who couldn't growl but barked his loudest) yet none of them could make Button-Bright hear. So, after vainly searching for the boy a full hour, they formed a procession and proceeded in the direction of the wicker castle of Ugu the Shoe-maker.

"Button-Bright's always getting lost," said Dorothy. "And, if he wasn't always getting found again, I'd prob'ly worry. He may have gone ahead of us, and he may have gone back; but, wherever he is, we'll find him sometime and somewhere, I'm almost sure."

Ugu the Shoemaker

CHAPTER 19

A curious thing about
Ugu the Shoemaker
was that he didn't
suspect, in the least,
that he was wicked. He wanted to be powerful
and great and he hoped to make himself master
of all the Land of Oz, that he might compel
everyone in that fairy country to obey him. His
ambition blinded him to the rights of others
and he imagined anyone else would act just as
he did if anyone else happened to be as clever
as himself.

When he inhabited his little shoemaking shop
in the City of Herku he had been discontented,
for a shoemaker is not looked upon with high
respect and Ugu knew that his ancestors had
been famous magicians for many centuries past

and therefore his family was above the ordinary. Even his father practiced magic, when Ugu was a boy; but his father had wandered away from Herku and had never come back again. So, when Ugu grew up, he was forced to make shoes for a living, knowing nothing of the magic of his forefathers. But one day, in searching through the attic of his house, he discovered all the books of magical recipes and many magical instruments which had formerly been in use in his family. From that day he stopped making shoes and began to study magic. Finally he aspired to become the greatest magician in Oz, and for days and weeks and months he thought on a plan to render all the other sorcerers and wizards, as well as those with fairy powers, helpless to oppose him.

From the books of his ancestors he learned the following facts:

(1) That Ozma of Oz was the fairy ruler of the Emerald City and the Land of Oz, and that she could not be destroyed by any magic ever devised. Also, by means of her Magic Picture she would be able to discover anyone who approached her royal palace with the idea of conquering it.

(2) That Glinda the Good was the most powerful Sorceress in Oz, among her other magical possessions being the Great Book of Records, which told her all that happened any-

where in the world. This Book of Records was very dangerous to Ugu's plans and Glinda was in the service of Ozma and would use her arts of sorcery to protect the girl Ruler.

(3) That the Wizard of Oz, who lived in Ozma's palace, had been taught much powerful magic by Glinda and had a bag of magic tools with which he might be able to conquer the Shoemaker.

(4) That there existed in Oz—in the Yip Country—a jeweled dishpan made of gold, which dishpan possessed marvelous powers of magic. At a magic word, which Ugu learned from the book, the dishpan would grow large enough for a man to sit inside it. Then, when he grasped both the golden handles, the dishpan would transport him in an instant to any place he wished to go within the borders of the Land of Oz.

No one now living, except Ugu, knew of the powers of this Magic Dishpan; so, after long study, the shoemaker decided that if he could manage to secure the dishpan he could, by its means, rob Ozma and Glinda and the Wizard of Oz of all their magic, thus becoming himself the most powerful person in all the land.

His first act was to go away from the City of Herku and build for himself the Wicker Castle in the hills. Here he carried his books and instruments of magic and here for a full year he diligently practiced all the magical arts learned from his ancestors. At the end of that time he could do a good many wonderful things.

Then, when all his preparations were made, he set out for the Yip Country and climbing the steep mountain at night he entered the house of Cayke the Cookie Cook and stole her diamond-studded gold dishpan while all the Yips were asleep. Taking his prize outside, he set the pan upon the ground and uttered the required magic word. Instantly the dishpan grew as large as a big washtub and Ugu seated himself in it and grasped the two handles. Then he wished himself in the great drawing-room of Glinda the Good.

He was there in a flash. First he took the Great Book of Records and put it in the dishpan. Then he went to Glinda's laboratory and took all her rare chemical compounds and her instruments of sorcery, placing these also in the dishpan, which he caused to grow large enough to hold them. Next he seated himself amongst the treasures he had stolen and wished himself in the room in Ozma's palace which the Wizard occupied and where he kept his bag of magic tools. This bag Ugu added to his plunder and then wished himself in the apartments of Ozma.

Here he first took the Magic Picture from the wall and then seized all tht other magical things which Ozma possessed. Having placed these in the dishpan he was about to climb in himself when he looked up and saw Ozma standing beside him. Her fairy instinct had warned her that danger was threatening her, so the beautiful girl Ruler rose from her couch and leaving her bedchamber at once confronted the thief.

Ugu had to think quickly, for he realized that if he permitted Ozma to rouse the inmates of her palace all his plans and his present successes were likely to come to naught. So he threw a scarf over the girl's head, so she could not scream, and pushed her into the dishpan and tied her fast, so she could not move. Then he climbed in beside her and wished himself in his own wicker castle. The Magic Dishpan was there in an instant, with all its contents, and Ugu rubbed his hands together in triumphant joy as he realized that he now possessed all the important magic in the Land of Oz and could force all the inhabitants of that fairyland to do as he willed.

So quickly had his journey been accomplished that before daylight the robber magician had locked Ozma in a room, making her a prisoner, and had unpacked and arranged all his stolen goods. The next day he placed the Book of Records on his table and hung the Magic Picture on his wall and put away in his cupboards and drawers all the elixirs and magic compounds he had stolen. The magical instruments he polished and arranged, and this was fascinating work and

made him very happy. The only thing that bothered him was Ozma. By turns the imprisoned Ruler wept and scolded the Shoemaker, haughtily threatening him with dire punishment for the wicked deeds he had done. Ugu became somewhat afraid of his fairy prisoner, in spite of the fact that he believed he had robbed her of all her powers; so he performed an enchantment that quickly disposed of her and placed her out of his sight and hearing. After that, being occupied with other things, he soon forgot her.

But now, when he looked into the Magic Picture and read the Great Book of Records, the Shoemaker learned that his wickedness was not to go unchallenged. Two important expeditions had set out to find him and force him to give up his stolen property. One was the party headed by the Wizard and Dorothy, while the other consisted of Cayke and the Frogman. Other

were also searching, but not in the right places. These two groups, however, were headed straight for the wicker castle and so Ugu began to plan how best to meet them and to defeat their efforts to conquer him.

More Surprises

CHAPTER 20

ALL that first day
after the union of
the two parties our
friends marched
steadily toward the wicker castle of Ugu the
Shoemaker. When night came they camped in
a little grove and passed a pleasant evening together, although some of them were worried
because Button-Bright was still lost.

"Perhaps," said Toto, as the animals lay
grouped together for the night, "this Shoemaker who stole my growl, and who stole Ozma
has also stolen Button Bright."

"How do you know that the Shoemaker stole
your growl?" demanded the Woozy.

"He has stolen about everything else of value
in Oz, hasn't he?" replied the dog.

"He has stolen everything he wants, perhaps," agreed the Lion; "but what could anyone want with your growl?"

"Well," said the dog, wagging his tail slowly, "my recollection is that it was a wonderful growl, soft and low and—and—"

"And ragged at the edges," said the Sawhorse.

"So," continued Toto, "if that magician hadn't any growl of his own, he might have wanted mine and stolen it."

"And, if he has, he will soon wish he hadn't," remarked the Mule. "Also, if he has stolen Button-Bright he will be sorry."

"Don't you like Button-Bright, then?" asked the Lion in surprise.

"It isn't a question of liking him," replied the Mule. "It's a question of watching him and looking after him. Any boy who causes his friends so much worry isn't worth having around. I never get lost."

"If you did," said Toto, "no one would worry a bit. I think Button-Bright is a very lucky boy, because he always gets found."

"See here," said the Lion, "this chatter is keeping us all awake and to-morrow is likely to be a busy day. Go to sleep and forget your quarrels."

"Friend Lion," retorted the dog, "if I hadn't lost my growl you would hear it now. I have as much right to talk as you have to sleep."

The Lion sighed.

"If only you had lost your voice, when you lost your growl," said he, "you would be a more agreeable companion."

But they quieted down, after that, and soon the entire camp was wrapped in slumber.

Next morning they made an early start but had hardly proceeded on their way an hour when, on climbing a slight elevation, they beheld in the distance a low mountain, on top of which stood Ugu's wicker castle. It was a good-sized building and rather pretty because the sides, roofs and domes were all of wicker closely woven, as it is in fine baskets.

"I wonder if it is strong?" said Dorothy musingly, as she eyed the queer castle.

"I suppose it is, since a magician built it," answered the Wizard. "With magic to protect it, even a paper castle might be as strong as if made of stone. This Ugu must be a man of ideas, because he does things in a different way from other people."

"Yes; no one else would steal our dear Ozma," sighed tiny Trot.

"I wonder if Ozma is there?" said Betsy, indicating the castle with a nod of her head.

"Where else could she be?" asked Scraps.

"S'pose we ask the Pink Bear," suggested Dorothy.

That seemed a good idea, so they halted the procession and the Bear King held the little Pink Bear on his lap and turned the crank in its side and asked:

"Where is Ozma of Oz?"

And the little Pink Bear answered:

"She is in a hole in the ground, a half mile away, at your left."

"Good gracious!" cried Dorothy. "Then she is not in Ugu's castle at all."

"It is lucky we asked that question," said the Wizard; "for, if we can find Ozma and rescue her, there will be no need for us to fight that wicked and dangerous magician."

"Indeed!" said Cayke. "Then what about my dishpan?"

The Wizard looked puzzled at her tone of remonstrance, so she added:

"Didn't you people from the Emerald City promise that we would all stick together, and that you would help me to get my dishpan if I would help you to get your Ozma? And didn't I bring to you the little Pink Bear, which has told you where Ozma is hidden?"

"She's right," said Dorothy to the Wizard. "We must do as we agreed."

"Well, first of all, let us go and rescue Ozma," proposed the Wizard. "Then our beloved Ruler may be able to advise us how to conquer Ugu the Shoemaker."

So they turned to the left and marched for half a mile until they came to a small but deep hole in the ground. At once all rushed to the brim to peer into the hole, but instead of finding there Princess Ozma of Oz, all that they saw was Button-Bright, who was lying asleep on the bottom.

Their cries soon wakened the boy, who sat up and rubbed his eyes. When he recognized his friends he smiled sweetly, saying: "Found again!"

"Where is Ozma?" inquired Dorothy anxiously.

"I don't know," answered Button-Bright from the depths of the hole. "I got lost, yesterday, as you may remember, and in the night, while I was wandering around in the moonlight, trying to find my way back to you, I suddenly fell into this hole."

"And wasn't Ozma in it then?"

"There was no one in it but me, and I was sorry it wasn't entirely empty. The sides are so steep I can't climb out, so there was nothing to be done but sleep until someone found me. Thank you for coming. If you'll please let down a rope I'll empty this hole in a hurry."

"How strange!" said Dorothy, greatly disappointed. "It's evident the Pink Bear didn't tell us the truth."

"He never makes a mistake," declared the

Lavender Bear King, in a tone that showed his feelings were hurt. And then he turned the crank of the little Pink Bear again and asked: "Is this the hole that Ozma of Oz is in?"

"Yes," answered the Pink Bear.

"That settles it," said the King, positively. "Your Ozma is in this hole in the ground."

"Don't be silly," returned Dorothy impatiently. "Even your beady eyes can see there is no one in the hole but Button-Bright."

"Perhaps Button-Bright is Ozma," suggested the King.

"And perhaps he isn't! Ozma is a girl, and Button-Bright is a boy."

"Your Pink Bear must be out of order," said the Wizard; "for, this time at least, his machinery has caused him to make an untrue statement."

The Bear King was so angry at this remark that he turned away, holding the Pink Bear in his paws, and refused to discuss the matter in any further way.

"At any rate," said the Frogman, "the Pink Bear has led us to your boy friend and so enabled you to rescue him."

Scraps was leaning so far over the hole, trying to find Ozma in it, that suddenly she lost her balance and pitched in headforemost. She fell upon Button-Bright and tumbled him over, but he was not hurt by her soft stuffed body and only laughed at the mishap. The Wizard buckled some straps together and let one end of them down into the hole, and soon both Scraps and the boy had climbed up and were standing safely beside the others.

They looked once more for Ozma, but the hole was now absolutely vacant. It was a round hole, so from the top they could plainly see every part of it. Before they left the place Dorothy went to the Bear King and said:

"I'm sorry we couldn't believe what the little Pink Bear said, 'cause we don't want to make you feel bad by doubting him. There must be a mistake, somewhere, and we prob'ly don't understand just what the little Pink Bear means. Will you let me ask him one more question?"

The Lavender Bear King was a good-natured bear, considering how he was made and stuffed and jointed, so he accepted Dorothy's apology and turned the crank and allowed the little girl to question his wee Pink Bear.

"Is Ozma *really* in this hole?" asked Dorothy.

"No," said the little Pink Bear.

This surprised everybody. Even the Bear King was now puzzled by the contradictory statements of his oracle.

"Where *is* she?" asked the King.

"Here, among you," answered the little Pink Bear.

"Well," said Dorothy, "this beats me, entirely! I guess the little Pink Bear has gone crazy."

"Perhaps," called Scraps, who was rapidly turning "cart-wheels" all around the perplexed group, "Ozma is invisible."

"Of course!" cried Betsy. "That would account for it."

"Well, I've noticed that people can speak, even when they've been made invisible," said the Wizard. And then he looked all around him and said in a solemn voice: "Ozma, are you here?"

There was no reply. Dorothy asked the question, too, and so did Button-Bright and Trot and Betsy; but none received any reply at all.

"It's strange—it's terrible strange!" muttered Cayke the Cookie Cook. "I was sure that the little Pink Bear always tells the truth."

"I still believe in his hontsty," said the Frogman, and this tribute so pleased the Bear King that he gave these last speakers grateful looks, but still gazed sourly on the others.

"Come to think of it," remarked the Wizard, "Ozma couldn't be invisible, for she is a fairy and fairies cannot be made invisible against their will. Of course she could be imprisoned by the magician, or even enchanted, or transformed, in spite of her fairy powers; but Ugu could not render her invisible by any magic at his command."

"I wonder if she's been transformed into Button-Bright?" said Dorothy nervously. Then she looked steadily at the boy and asked: "Are you Ozma? Tell me truly!"

Button-Bright laughed.

"You're getting rattled, Dorothy," he replied. "Nothing ever enchants *me*. If I were Ozma, do you think I'd have tumbled into that hole?"

"Anyhow," said the Wizard, "Ozma would never try to deceive her friends, or prevent them from recognizing her, in whatever form she happened to be. The puzzle is still a puzzle, so let us go on to the wicker castle and question the magician himself. Since it was he who stole our Ozma, Ugu is the one who must tell us where to find her."

Magic Against Magic

CHAPTER 21

THE Wizard's ad-
vice was good, so
again they started in
the direction of the
low mountain on the crest of which the wicker
castle had been built. They had been gradually
advancing up hill, so now the elevation seemed
to them more like a round knoll than a mountain-top. However, the sides of the knoll were
sloping and covered with green grass, so there
was a stiff climb before them yet.

Undaunted, they plodded on and had almost
reached the knoll when they suddenly observed
that it was surrounded by a circle of flame. At
first the flames barely rose above the ground, but
presently they grew higher and higher until a
circle of flaming tongues of fire taller than any

of their heads quite surrounded the hill on which the wicker castle stood. When they approached the flames the heat was so intense that it drove them back again.

"This will never do for me!" exclaimed the Patchwork Girl. "I catch fire very easily."

"It won't do for me, either," grumbled the Sawhorse, prancing to the rear.

"I also object strongly to fire," said the Bear King, following the Sawhorse to a safe distance and hugging the little Pink Bear with his paws.

"I suppose the foolish Shoemaker imagines these blazes will stop us," remarked the Wizard, with a smile of scorn for Ugu. "But I am able to inform you that this is merely a simple magic trick which the robber stole from Glinda the Good, and by good fortune I know how to destroy these flames, as well as how to produce them. Will some one of you kindly give me a match?"

You may be sure the girls carried no matches, nor did the Frogman or Cayke or any of the animals. But Button-Bright, after searching carefully through his pockets, which contained all sorts of useful and useless things, finally produced a match and handed it to the Wizard, who tied it to the end of a branch which he tore from a small tree growing near them. Then the little Wizard carefully lighted the match and running forward thrust it into the nearest flame.

Instantly the circle of fire began to die away and soon vanished completely, leaving the way clear for them to proceed.

"That was funny!" laughed Button-Bright.

"Yes," agreed the Wizard, "it seems odd that a little match could destroy such a great circle of fire, but when Glinda invented this trick she believed no one would ever think of a match being a remedy for fire. I suppose even Ugu doesn't know how we managed to quench the flames of his barrier, for only Glinda and I know the secret. Glinda's Book of Magic, which Ugu stole, told how to make the flames, but not how to put them out."

They now formed in marching order and proceeded to advance up the slope of the hill; but had not gone far when before them rose a wall of steel, the surface of which was thickly covered with sharp, gleaming points resembling daggers. The wall completely surrounded the wicker castle and its sharp points prevented anyone from climbing it. Even the Patchwork Girl might be ripped to pieces if she dared attempt it.

"Ah!" exclaimed the Wizard cheerfully, "Ugu is now using one of my own tricks against me. But this is more serious than the Barrier of Fire, because the only way to destroy the wall is to get on the other side of it."

"How can that be done?" asked Dorothy.

The Wizard looked thoughtfully around his

little party and his face grew troubled.

"It's a pretty high wall," he sadly remarked. "I'm pretty sure the Cowardly Lion could not leap over it."

"I'm sure of that, too!" said the Lion with a shudder of fear. "If I foolishly tried such a leap I would be caught on those dreadful spikes."

"I think I could do it, sir," said the Frogman, with a bow to the Wizard. "It is an up-hill jump, as well as being a high jump, but I'm considered something of a jumper by my friends in the Yip Country and I believe a good strong leap will carry me to the other side."

"I'm sure it would," agreed the Cookie Cook.

"Leaping, you know, is a froglike accomplishment," continued the Frogman, modestly, "but please tell me what I am to do when I reach the other side of the wall."

"You're a brave creature," said the Wizard, admiringly. "Has anyone a pin?"

Betsy had one, which she gave him.

"All you need do," said the Wizard to the Frogman, giving him the pin, "is to stick this into the other side of the wall."

"But the wall is of steel!" exclaimed the big frog.

"I know; at least, it *seems* to be steel; but do as I tell you. Stick the pin into the wall and it will disappear."

The Frogman took off his handsome coat and

carefully folded it and laid it on the grass. Then he removed his hat and laid it, together with his goldheaded cane, beside the coat. He then went back a way and made three powerful leaps, in rapid succession. The first two leaps took him to the wall and the third leap carried him well over it, to the amazement of all. For a short time he disappeared from their view, but when he had obeyed the Wizard's injunction and had thrust the pin into the wall, the huge barrier vanished and showed them the form of the Frogman, who now went to where his coat lay and put it on again.

"We thank you very much," said the delighted Wizard. "That was the most wonderful leap I ever saw and it has saved us from defeat by our enemy. Let us now hurry on to the castle before Ugu the Shoemaker thinks of some other means to stop us."

"We must have surprised him, so far," declared Dorothy.

"Yes, indeed. The fellow knows a lot of magic —all of our tricks and some of his own," replied the Wizard. "So, if he is half as clever as he ought to be, we shall have trouble with him yet."

He had scarcely spoken these words when out from the gates of the wicker castle marched a regiment of soldiers, clad in gay uniforms and all bearing long, pointed spears and sharp battle-axes. These soldiers were girls, and the uniforms were short skirts of yellow and black satin, golden shoes, bands of gold across their foreheads and necklaces of glittering jewels. Their jackets were scarlet, braided with silver cords. There were hundreds of these girl-soldiers, and they were more terrible than beautiful, being strong and fierce in appearance. They formed a circle all around the castle and faced outward, their spears pointed toward the invaders and their battle-axes held over their shoulders ready to strike.

Of course our friends halted at once, for they had not expected this dreadful array of soldiery. The Wizard seemed puzzled and his companions exchanged discouraged looks.

"I'd no idea Ugu had such an army as that," said Dorothy. "The castle doesn't look big enough to hold them all."

"It isn't," declared the Wizard.

"But they all marched out of it."

"They seemed to; but I don't believe it is a real army at all. If Ugu the Shoemaker had so many people living with him, I'm sure the Czarover of Herku would have mentioned the fact to us."

"They're only girls!" laughed Scraps.

"Girls are the fiercest soldiers of all," declared the Frogman. "They are more brave than men and they have better nerves. That is probably why the magician uses them for soldiers and has sent them to oppose us."

No one argued this statement, for all were staring hard at the line of soldiers, which now, having taken a defiant position, remained motionless.

"Here is a trick of magic to me," admitted the Wizard, after a time. "I do not believe the army is real, but the spears may be sharp enough to prick us, nevertheless, so we must be cautious. Let us take time to consider how to meet this difficulty."

While they were thinking it over Scraps danced closer to the line of girl soldiers. Her button eyes sometimes saw more than did the natural eyes of her comrades and so, after staring hard at the magician's army, she boldly advanced and danced right through the threatening line! On the other side she waved her stuffed arms and called out:

"Come on, folks. The spears can't hurt you."

"Ah!" said the Wizard, gayly, "an optical illusion, as I thought. Let us all follow the Patchwork Girl."

The three little girls were somewhat nervous in attempting to brave the spears and battle-axes, but after the others had safely passed the line they ventured to follow. And, when all had passed through the ranks of the girl army, the army itself magically disappeared from view.

All this time our friends had been getting farther up the hill and nearer to the wicker cas-

tle. Now, continuing their advance, they expected something else to oppose their way, but to their astonishment nothing happened and presently they arrived at the wicker gates, which stood wide open, and boldly entered the domain of Ugu the Shoemaker.

In the Wicker Castle

CHAPTER 22

NO sooner were the Wizard of Oz and his followers well within the castle entrance when the big gates swung to with a clang and heavy bars dropped across them. They looked at one another uneasily, but no one cared to speak of the incident. If they were indeed prisoners in the wicker castle it was evident they must find a way to escape, but their first duty was to attend to the errand on which they had come and seek the Royal Ozma, whom they believed to be a prisoner of the magician, and rescue her.

They found they had entered a square courtyard, from which an entrance led into the main building of the castle. No person had appeared to greet them, so far, although a gaudy peacock, perched upon the wall, cackled with laughter and said in its sharp, shrill voice: "Poor fools! Poor fools!"

"I hope the peacock is mistaken," remarked the Frogman, but no one else paid any attention to the bird. They were a little awed by the stillness and loneliness of the place.

As they entered the doors of the castle, which stood invitingly open, these also closed behind them and huge bolts shot into place. The animals had all accompanied the party into the castle, because they felt it would be dangerous for them to separate. They were forced to follow a zigzag passage, turning this way and that, until finally they entered a great central hall, circular in form and with a high dome from which was suspended an enormous chandelier.

The Wizard went first, and Dorothy, Betsy and Trot followed him, Toto keeping at the heels of his little mistress. Then came the Lion, the Woozy and the Sawhorse; then Cayke the Cookie Cook and Button-Bright; then the Lavender Bear carrying the Pink Bear, and finally the Frogman and the Patchwork Girl, with Hank the Mule tagging behind. So it was the Wizard who caught the first glimpse of the big domed hall, but the others quickly followed and gathered in a wondering group just within the entrance.

Upon a raised platform at one side was a heavy table on which lay Glinda's Great Book of Records; but the platform was firmly fastened to the floor and the table was fastened to the platform and the Book was chained fast to the table—just as it had been when it was kept in Glinda's palace. On the wall over the table hung Ozma's Magic Picture. On a row of shelves at the opposite side of the hall stood all the chemicals and essences of magic and all the magical instruments that had been stolen from Glinda and Ozma and the Wizard, with glass doors covering the shelves so that no one could get at them.

And in a far corner at Ugu the Shoemaker, his feet lazily extended, his skinny hands clasped behind his head. He was leaning back at his ease and calmly smoking a long pipe. Around the magician was a sort of cage, seemingly made of golden bars set wide apart, and at his feet—also within the cage—reposed the long-sought diamond-studded dishpan of Cayke the Cookie Cook.

Princess Ozma of Oz was nowhere to be seen.

"Well, well," said Ugu, when the invaders had stood in silence for a moment, staring about them, "this visit is an expected pleasure, I assure you. I knew you were coming and I know why you are here. You are not welcome, for I cannot use any of you to my advantage, but as you have insisted on coming I hope you will make the afternoon call as brief as possible. It won't take long to transact your business with me. You will ask me for Ozma, and my reply will be that you may find her—if you can."

"Sir," answered the Wizard, in a tone of rebuke, "you are a very wicked and cruel person. I suppose you imagine, because you have stolen this poor woman's dishpan and all the best magic in Oz, that you are more powerful than we are and will be able to triumph over us."

"Yes," said Ugu the Shoemaker, slowly filling his pipe with fresh tobacco from a silver bowl that stood beside him, "that is exactly what I imagine. It will do you no good to demand from me the girl who was formerly the Ruler of Oz, because I will not tell you where I have hidden her—and you can't guess in a thousand years. Neither will I restore to you any of the magic I have captured. I am not so foolish. But bear this in mind: I mean to be the Ruler of Oz myself, hereafter, so I advise you to be careful how you address your future Monarch."

"Ozma is still Ruler of Oz, wherever you may have hidden her," declared the Wizard. "And bear this in mind, miserable Shoemaker: We intend to find her and to rescue her, in time, but our first duty and pleasure will be to conquer you and then punish you for your misdeeds."

"Very well; go ahead and conquer," said Ugu. "I'd really like to see how you can do it."

Now, although the little Wizard had spoken so boldly, he had at the moment no idea how they might conquer the magician. He had that morning given the Frogman, at his request, a dose of zosozo from his bottle, and the Frogman had promised to fight a good fight if it was necessary; but the Wizard knew that strength alone could not avail against magical arts. The toy Bear King seemed to have some pretty good magic, however, and the Wizard depended to an extent on that. But something ought to be done right away, and the Wizard didn't know what it was.

While he considered this perplexing question and the others stood looking at him as their leader, a queer thing happened. The floor of the great circular hall, on which they were standing, suddenly began to tip. Instead of being flat and level it became a slant, and the slant grew steeper and steeper until none of the party could manage to stand upon it. Presently they all slid down to the wall, which was now under them, and then it became evident that the whole vast room was slowly turning upside down! Only Ugu the Shoemaker, kept in place by the bars of his golden cage, remained in his former position, and the wicked magician seemed to enjoy the surprise of his victims immensely.

First, they all slid down to the wall back of them, but as the room continued to turn over they next slid down the wall and found themselves at the bottom of the great dome, bumping against the big chandelier which, like everything else, was now upside-down.

The turning movement now stopped and the room became stationary. Looking far up, they saw Ugu suspended in his cage at the very top, which had once been the floor .

"Ah," said he, grinning down at them, "the way to conquer is to act, and he who acts promptly is sure to win. This makes a very good prison, from which I am sure you cannot escape. Please amuse yourselves in any way you like, but I must beg you to excuse me, as I have business in another part of my castle."

Saying this, he opened a trap door in the floor of his cage (which was now over his head) and climbed through it and disappeared from their view. The diamond dishpan still remained in the cage, but the bars kept it from falling down on their heads.

"Well, I declare!" said the Patchwork Girl, seizing one of the bars of the chandelier and swinging from it, "we must peg one for the Shoemaker, for he has trapped us very cleverly."

"Get off my foot, please," said the Lion to the Sawhorse.

"And oblige me, Mr. Mule," remarked the

Woozy, "by taking your tail out of my left eye."

"It's rather crowded down here," explained Dorothy, "because the dome is rounding and we have all slid into the middle of it. But let us keep as quiet as possible until we can think what's best to be done."

"Dear, dear!" wailed Cayke; "I wish I had my darling dishpan," and she held her arms longingly toward it.

"I wish I had the magic on those shelves up there," sighed the Wizard.

"Don't you s'pose we could get to it?" asked Trot anxiously.

"We'd have to fly," laughed the Patchwork Girl.

But the Wizard took the suggestion seriously, and so did the Frogman. They talked it over and soon planned an attempt to reach the shelves where the magical instruments were. First the Frogman lay against the rounding dome and braced his foot on the stem of the chandelier; then the Wizard climbed over him and lay on the dome with his feet on the Frogman's shoulders; the Cookie Cook came next; then Button-Bright climbed to the woman's shoulders; then Dorothy climbed up, and Betsy and Trot, and finally the Patchwork Girl, and all their lengths made a long line that reached far up the dome but not far enough for Scraps to touch the shelves.

"Wait a minute; perhaps I can reach the magic; called the Bear King, and began scrambling up the bodies of the others. But when he came to the Cookie Cook his soft paws tickled her side so that she squirmed and upset the whole line. Down they came, tumbling in a heap against the animals, and although no one was much hurt it was a bad mix-up and the Frogman, who was at the bottom, almost lost his temper before he could get on his feet again.

Cayke positively refused to try what she called "the pyramid act" again, and as the Wizard was now convinced they could not reach the magic tools in that manner the attempt was abandoned.

"But *something* must be done," said the Wizard, and then he turned to the Lavender Bear and asked: "Cannot Your Majesty's magic help us to escape from here?"

"My magic powers are limited," was the reply. "When I was stuffed, the fairies stood by and slyly dropped some magic into my stuffing. Therefore I can do any of the magic that's inside me, but nothing else. You, however, are a wizard, and a wizard should be able to do anything."

"Your Majesty forgets that my tools of magic have been stolen," said the Wizard sadly, "and a wizard without tools is as helpless as a carpenter without a hammer or saw."

"Don't give up," pleaded Button-Bright, " 'cause if we can't get out of this queer prison we'll all starve to death."

"Not I!" laughed the Patchwork Girl, now standing on top the chandelier, at the place that was meant to be the bottom of it.

"Don't talk of such dreadful things," said Trot, shuddering. "We came here to capture the Shoemaker, didn't we?"

"Yes, and to save Ozma," said Betsy.

"And here we are, captured ourselves, and my darling dishpan up there in plain sight!" wailed the Cookie Cook, wiping her eyes on the tail of the Frogman's coat.

"Hush!" called the Lion, with a low, deep growl. "Give the Wizard time to think."

"He has plenty of time," said Scraps. "What he needs is the Scarecrow's brains."

After all, it was little Dorothy who came to their rescue, and her ability to save them was almost as much a surprise to the girl as it was to her friends. Dorothy had been secretly testing the powers of her Magic Belt, which she had once captured from the Nome King, and experimenting with it in various ways, ever since she had started on this eventful journey. At different times she had stolen away from the others of her party and in solitude had tried to find out what the Magic Belt could do and what it could not do. There were a lot of things it could not do, she discovered, but she learned some things about the Belt which even her girl friends did not suspect she knew.

For one thing, she had remembered that when the Nome King owned it the Magic Belt used to perform transformations, and by thinking hard she had finally recalled the way in which such transformations had been accomplished. Better than this, however, was the discovery that the Magic Belt would grant its wearer one wish a day. All she need do was close her right eye and wiggle her left toe and then draw a long breath and make her wish. Yesterday she had wished in secret for a box of caramels, and instantly found the box beside her. To-day she had saved her daily wish, in case she might need it in an emergency, and the time had now come when she must use the wish to enable her to escape with her friends from the prison in which Ugu had caught them.

So, without telling anyone what she intended to do—for she had only used the wish once and could not be certain how powerful the Magic Belt might be—Dorothy closed her right eye and wiggled her left big toe and drew a long breath and wished with all her might. The next moment the room began to revolve again, as slowly as before, and by degrees they all slid to the side wall and down the wall to the floor —all but Scraps, who was so astonished that she still clung to the chandelier. When the big hall was in its proper position again and the others

stood firmly upon the floor of it, they looked far up to the dome and saw the Patchwork Girl swinging from the chandelier.

"Good gracious!" cried Dorothy. "How ever will you get down?"

"Won't the room keep turning?" asked Scraps.

"I hope not. I believe it has stopped for good," said Princess Dorothy.

"Then stand from under, so you won't get hurt!" shouted the Patchwork Girl, and as soon as they had obeyed this request she let go the chandelier and came tumbling down heels over head and twisting and turning in a very exciting manner. Plump! she fell on the tiled floor and they ran to her and rolled her and patted her into shape again.

The Defiance of Ugu the Shoemaker

CHAPTER 23

THE delay caused by Scraps had prevented anyone from running to the shelves to secure the magic instruments so badly needed. Even Cayke neglected to get her diamond-studded dishpan because she was watching the Patchwork Girl. And now the magician had opened his trap door and appeared in his golden cage again, frowning angrily because his prisoners had been able to turn their upside-down prison right-side-up.

"Which of you has dared defy my magic?" he shouted in a terrible voice.

"It was I," answered Dorothy calmly.

"Then I shall destroy you, for you are only an Earth girl and no fairy," he said, and began to mumble some magic words.

Dorothy now realized that Ugu must be treated as an enemy, so she advanced toward the corner in which he sat, saying as she went:

"I am not afraid of you, Mr. Shoemaker, and I think you'll be sorry, pretty soon, that you're such a bad man. You can't destroy me and I won't destroy you, but I'm going to punish you for your wickedness."

Ugu laughed a laugh that was not nice to hear, and then he waved his hand. Dorothy was halfway across the room when suddenly a wall of glass rose before her and stopped her progress. Through the glass she could see the magician sneering at her because she was a weak little girl, and this provoked her. Although the glass wall obliged her to halt she instantly pressed both hands to her Magic Belt and cried in a loud voice:

"Ugu the Shoemaker, by the magic virtues of the Magic Belt, I command you to become a dove!"

The magician instantly realized he was being enchanted, for he could feel his form changing. He struggled desperately against the enchantment, mumbling magic words and making magic passes with his hands. And in one way he succeeded in defeating Dorothy's purpose, for while his form soon changed to that of a gray dove, the dove was of an enormous size—bigger even than Ugu had been as a man—and this feat he had been able to accomplish before his powers of magic wholly deserted him.

And the dove was not gentle, as doves usually are, for Ugu was terribly enraged at the little girl's success. His books had told him nothing of the Nome King's Magic Belt, the Country of the Nomes being outside the Land of Oz. He knew, however, that he was likely to be conquered unless he made a fierce fight, so he spread his wings and rose in the air and flew directly toward Dorothy. The Wall of Glass had disappeared the instant Ugu became transformed.

Dorothy had meant to command the Belt to transform the magician into a Dove of Peace, but in her excitement she forgot to say more than "dove," and now Ugu was not a Dove of Peace by any means, but rather a spiteful Dove of War. His size made his sharp beak and claws very dangerous, but Dorothy was not afraid when he came darting toward her with his talons outstretched and his sword-like beak open. She knew the Magic Belt would protect its wearer from harm.

But the Frogman did not know that fact and became alarmed at the little girl's seeming danger. So he gave a sudden leap and leaped full upon the back of the great dove.

Then began a desperate struggle. The dove

was as strong as Ugu had been, and in size it was considerably bigger than the Frogman. But the Frogman had eaten the zosozo and it had made him fully as strong as Ugu the Dove. At the first leap he bore the dove to the floor, but the giant bird got free and began to bite and claw the Frogman, beating him down with its great wings whenever he attempted to rise. The thick, tough skin of the big frog was not easily damaged, but Dorothy feared for her champion and by again using the transformation power of the Magic Belt she made the dove grow small, until it was no larger than a canary bird.

Ugu had not lost his knowledge of magic when he lost his shape as a man, and he now realized it was hopeless to oppose the power of the Magic Belt and knew that his only hope of escape lay in instant action. So he quickly flew into the golden jeweled dishpan he had stolen from Cayke the Cookie Cook and, as birds can talk as well as beasts or men in the Fairyland of Oz, he muttered the magic word that was required and wished himself in the Country of the Quadlings—which was as far away from the wicker castle as he believed he could get.

Our friends did not know, of course, what Ugu was about to do. They saw the dishpan tremble an instant and then disappear, the dove disappearing with it, and although they waited expectantly for some minutes for the magician's return, Ugu did not come back again.

"Seems to me," said the Wizard in a cheerful voice, "that we have conquered the wicked magician more quickly than we expected to."

"Don't say 'we'—Dorothy did it!" cried the Patchwork Girl, turning three somersaults in succession and then walking around on her hands. "Hurrah for Dorothy!"

"I thought you said you did not know how to use the magic of the Nome King's Belt," said the Wizard to Dorothy.

"I didn't know, at that time," she replied, "but afterward I remembered how the Nome King once used the Magic Belt to enchant people and transform 'em into ornaments and all sorts of things; so I tried some enchantments in secret and after a while I transformed the Sawhorse into a potato-masher and back again, and the Cowardly Lion into a pussycat and back again, and then I knew the thing would work all right."

"When did you perform those enchantments?" asked the Wizard, much surprised.

"One night when all the rest of you were asleep but Scraps, and she had gone chasing moonbeams."

"Well," remarked the Wizard, "your discovery has certainly saved us a lot of trouble, and we must all thank the Frogman, too, for making such a good fight. The dove's shape had Ugu's evil disposition inside it, and that made the monster bird dangerous."

The Frogman was looking sad because the bird's talons had torn his pretty clothes, but he bowed with much dignity at this well-deserved praise. Cayke, however, had squatted on the floor and was sobbing bitterly.

"My precious dishpan is gone!" she wailed. "Gone, just as I had found it again!"

"Never mind," said Trot, trying to comfort her, "it's sure to be *some*where, so we'll cert'nly run across it some day."

"Yes, indeed," added Betsy; "now that we have Ozma's Magic Picture, we can tell just where the Dove went with your dishpan."

They all approached the Magic Picture, and Dorothy wished it to show the enchanted form of Ugu the Shoemaker, wherever it might be. At once there appeared in the frame of the Picture a scene in the far Quadling Country, where the Dove was perched disconsolately on the limb of a tree and the jeweled dishpan lay on the ground just underneath the limb.

"But where is the place—how far or how near?" asked Cayke anxiously.

"The Book of Records will tell us that," answered the Wizard. So they looked in the Great Book and read the following:

"Ugu the Magician, being transformed into a dove by Princess Dorothy of Oz, has used the magic of the golden dishpan to carry him instantly to the northeast corner of the Quadling Country."

"That's all right," said Dorothy. "Don't worry, Cayke, for the Scarecrow and the Tin Woodman are in that part of the country, looking for Ozma, and they'll surely find your dishpan."

"Good gracious!" exclaimed Button-Bright, "we've forgot all about Ozma. Let's find out where the magician hid her."

Back to the Magic Picture they trooped, but when they wished to see Ozma, wherever she might be hidden, only a round black spot appeared in the center of the canvas.

"I don't see how *that* can be Ozma!" said Dorothy, much puzzled.

"It seems to be the best the Magic Picture can do, however," said the Wizard, no less surprised. "If it's an enchantment, it looks as if the magician had transformed Ozma into a chunk of pitch."

The Little Pink Bear Speaks Truly

CHAPTER 24

FOR several minutes
they all stood staring
at the black spot on
the canvas of the
Magic Picture, wondering what it could mean.

"P'r'aps we'd better ask the little Pink Bear
about Ozma," suggested Trot.

"Pshaw!" said Button-Bright, "*he* don't know
anything."

"He never makes a mistake," declared the
King.

"He did once, surely," said Betsy. "But perhaps he wouldn't make a mistake again."

"He won't have the chance," grumbled the
Bear King.

"We might hear what he has to say," said
Dorothy. "It won't do any harm to ask the Pink

Bear where Ozma is."

"I will not have him questioned," declared the King, in a surly voice. "I do not intend to allow my little Pink Bear to be again insulted by your foolish doubts. He never makes a mistake."

"Didn't he say Ozma was in that hole in the ground?" asked Betsy.

"He did; and I am certain she was there," replied the Lavender Bear.

Scraps laughed jeeringly and the others saw there was no use arguing with the stubborn Bear King, who seemed to have absolute faith in his Pink Bear. The Wizard, who knew that magical things can usually be depended upon, and that the little Pink Bear was able to answer questions by some remarkable power of magic, thought it wise to apologize to the Lavender Bear for the unbelief of his friends, at the same time urging the King to consent to question the Pink Bear once more. Cayke and the Frogman also pleaded with the big Bear, who finally agreed, although rather ungraciously, to put the little Bear's wisdom to the test once more. So he sat the little one on his knee and turned the crank and the Wizard himself asked the questions in a very respectful tone of voice.

"Where is Ozma?" was his first query.

"Here, in this room," answered the little Pink Bear.

They all looked around the room, but of course did not see her.

"In what part of this room is she?" was the Wizard's next question.

"In Button-Bright's pocket," said the little Pink Bear.

This reply amazed them all, you may be sure, and although the three girls smiled and Scraps yelled: "Hoo-ray!" in derision, the Wizard seemed to consider the matter with grave thoughtfulness.

"In which one of Button-Bright's pockets is Ozma?" he presently inquired.

"In the lefthand jacket-pocket," said the little Pink Bear.

"The pink one has gone crazy!" exclaimed Button-Bright, staring hard at the little bear on the big bear's knee.

"I am not so sure of that," declared the Wizard. "If Ozma proves to be really in your pocket, then the little Pink Bear spoke truly when he said Ozma was in that hole in the ground. For at that time you were also in the hole, and after we had pulled you out of it the little Pink Bear said Ozma was not in the hole."

"He never makes a mistake," asserted the Bear King, stoutly.

"Empty that pocket, Button-Bright, and let's see what's in it," requested Dorothy.

So Button-Bright laid the contents of his left jacket-pocket on the table. These proved to be a peg-top, a bunch of string, a small rubber ball and a golden peach-pit.

"What's this?" asked the Wizard, picking up the peach-pit and examining it closely.

"Oh," said the boy, "I saved that to show to the girls, and then forgot all about it. It came out of a lonesome peach hat I found in the orchard back yonder, and which I ate while I was lost. It looks like gold, and I never saw a peach-pit like it before."

"Nor I," said the Wizard, "and that makes it seem suspicious."

All heads were bent over the golden peach-pit. The Wizard turned it over several times and then took out his pocket-knife and pried the pit open.

As the two halves fell apart a pink, cloud-like haze came pouring from the golden peach-pit, almost filling the big room, and from the haze a form took shape and settled beside them. Then, as the haze faded away, a sweet voice said: "Thank you, my friends!" and there before them stood their lovely girl Ruler, Ozma of Oz.

With a cry of delight Dorothy rushed forward and embraced her. Scraps turned gleeful flip-flops all around the room. Button-Bright gave a low whistle of astonishment. The Frogman took off his tall hat and bowed low before the beautiful girl who had been freed from her enchantment in so startling a manner.

For a time no sound was heard beyond the low murmur of delight that came from the amazed group, but presently the growl of the big Lavender Bear grew louder and he said in a tone of triumph:

"He never makes a mistake!"

CHAPTER 25

"IT'S funny," said Toto, standing before his friend the Lion and wagging his tail, "but I've found my growl at last! I am positive, now, that it was the cruel magician who stole it."

"Let's hear your growl," requested the Lion.

"Gr-r-r-r-r-r!" said Toto.

"That is fine," declared the big beast. "It isn't as loud or as deep as the growl of the big Lavender Bear, but it is a very respectable growl for a small dog. Where did you find it, Toto?"

"I was smelling in the corner, yonder," said Toto, "when suddenly a mouse ran out—and I growled!"

The others were all busy congratulating Ozma, who was very happy at being released

267

from the confinement of the golden peach-pit, where the magician had placed her with the notion that she never could be found or liberated.

"And only to think," cried Dorothy, "that Button-Bright has been carrying you in his pocket all this time, and we never knew it!"

"The little Pink Bear told you," said the Bear King, "but you wouldn't believe him."

"Never mind, my dears," said Ozma graciously; "all is well that ends well, and you couldn't be expected to know I was inside the peach-pit. Indeed, I feared I would remain a captive much longer than I did, for Ugu is a bold and clever magician and he had hidden me very securely."

"You were in a fine peach," said Button-Bright; "the best I ever ate."

"The magician was foolish to make the peach so tempting," remarked the Wizard; "but Ozma would lend beauty to any transformation."

"How did you manage to conquer Ugu the Shoemaker?" inquired the girl Ruler of Oz.

Dorothy started to tell the story and Trot helped her, and Button-Bright wanted to relate it in his own way, and the Wizard tried to make it clear to Ozma, and Betsy had to remind them of important things they left out, and all together there was such a chatter that it was a wonder that Ozma understood any of it. But she listened patiently, with a smile on her lovely face at their eagerness, and presently had gleaned all the details of their adventures.

Ozma thanked the Frogman very earnestly for his assistance and she advised Cayke the Cookie Cook to dry her weeping eyes, for she promised to take her to the Emerald City and see that her cherished dishpan was restored to her. Then the beautiful Ruler took a chain of emeralds from around her own neck and placed it around the neck of the little Pink Bear.

"Your wise answers to the questions of my friends," said she, "helped them to rescue me. Therefore I am deeply grateful to you and to your noble King."

The bead eyes of the little Pink Btar stared unresponsive to this praise until the Big Lavender Bear turned the crank in its side, when it said in its squeaky voice:

"I thank Your Majesty."

"For my part," returned the Bear King, "I realize that you were well worth saving, Miss Ozma, and so I am much pleased that we could be of service to you. By means of my Magic Wand I have been creating exact images of your Emerald City and your Royal Palace, and I must confess that they are more attractive than any places I have ever seen—not excepting Bear Center."

"I would like to entertain you in my palace," returned Ozma, sweetly, "and you are welcome to return with me and to make me a long visit, if your bear subjects can spare you from your own kingdom."

"As for that," answered the King, "my kingdom causes me little worry, and I often find it somewhat tame and uninteresting. Therefore I am in no hurry to return to it and will be glad to accept your kind invitation. Corporal Waddle may be trusted to care for my bears in my absence."

"And you'll bring the little Pink Bear?" asked Dorothy eagerly.

"Of course, my dear; I would not willingly part with him."

They remained in the wicker castle for three days, carefully packing all the magical things that had been stolen by Ugu and also taking whatever in the way of magic the shoemaker had inherited from his ancestors.

"For," said Ozma, "I have forbidden any of my subjects except Glinda the Good and the Wizard of Oz to practice magical arts, because they cannot be trusted to do good and not harm. Therefore Ugu must never again be permitted to work magic of any sort."

"Well," remarked Dorothy cheerfully, "a dove can't do much in the way of magic, anyhow, and I'm going to keep Ugu in the form of a dove until he reforms and becomes a good and honest shoemaker."

When everything was packed and loaded on the backs of the animals, they set out for the river, taking a more direct route than that by which Cayke and the Frogman had come. In this way they avoided the Cities of Thi and Herku and Bear Center and after a pleasant journey reached the Winkie River and found a jolly ferryman who had a fine big boat and was willing to carry the entire party by water to a place quite near to the Emerald City.

The river had many windings and many branches, and the journey did not end in a day, but finally the boat floated into a pretty lake which was but a short distance from Ozma's home. Here the jolly ferryman was rewarded for his labors and then the entire party set out in a grand procession to march to the Emerald City.

News that the Royal Ozma had been found spread quickly throughout the neighborhood and both sides of the road soon became lined with loyal subjects of the beautiful and beloved Ruler. Therefore Ozma's ears heard little but cheers and her eyes beheld little else than waving handkerchiefs and banners during all the triumphal march from the lake to the city's gates.

And there she met a still greater concourse, for all the inhabitants of the Emerald City turned out to welcome her return and several bands played gay music and all the houses were decorated with flags and bunting and never before were the people so joyous and happy as at this moment when they welcomed home their girl Ruler. For she had been lost and was now found again, and surely that was cause for rejoicing.

Glinda was at the royal palace to meet the returning party and the good Sorceress was indeed glad to have her Great Book of Records returned to her, as well as all the precious collection of magic instruments and elixirs and chemicals that had been stolen from her castle. Cap'n Bill and the Wizard at once hung the Magic Picture upon the wall of Ozma's boudoir and the Wizard was so light-hearted that he did several tricks with the tools in his black bag to amuse his companions and prove that once again he was a powerful wizard.

For a whole week there was feasting and merriment and all sorts of joyous festivities at the palace, in honor of Ozma's safe return. The Lavender Bear and the little Pink Bear received much attention and were honored by all, much to the Bear King's satisfaction. The Frogman speedily became a favorite at the Emerald City and the Shaggy Man and Tik-Tok and Jack Pumpkinhead, who had now returned from their search, were very polite to the big frog and made him feel quite at home. Even the Cookie Cook because she was a stranger and Ozma's guest

was shown as much deference as if she had been a queen.

"All the same, Your Majesty," said Cayke to Ozma, day after day, with tiresome repetition, "I hope you will soon find my jeweled dish-pan, for never can I be quite happy without it."

Dorothy Forgives

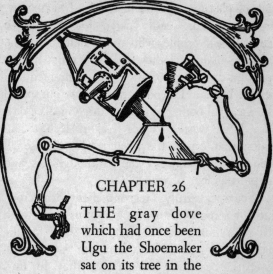

CHAPTER 26

THE gray dove
which had once been
Ugu the Shoemaker
sat on its tree in the
far Quadling Country and moped, chirping
dismally and brooding over its misfortunes.
After a time the Scarecrow and the Tin Woodman came along and sat beneath the tree, paying
no heed to the mutterings of the gray dove.

The Tin Woodman took a small oilcan from
his tin pocket and carefully oiled his tin joints
with it. While he was thus engaged the Scarecrow remarked:

"I feel much better, dear comrade, since we
found that heap of nice clean straw and you
stuffed me anew with it."

"And I feel much better now that my joints

are oiled," returned the Tin Woodman, with a sigh of pleasure. "You and I, friend Scarecrow, are much more easily cared for than those clumsy meat people, who spend half their time dressing in fine clothes and who must live in splendid dwellings in order to be contented and happy. You and I do not eat, and so we are spared the dreadful bother of getting three meals a day. Nor do we waste half our lives in sleep, a condition that causes the meat people to lose all consciousness and become as thoughtless and helpless as logs of wood."

"You speak truly," responded the Scarecrow, tucking some wisps of straw into his breast with his padded fingers. "I often feel sorry for the meat people, many of whom are my friends. Even the beasts are happier than they, for they require less to make them content. And the birds are the luckiest creatures of all, for they can fly swiftly where they will and find a home at any place they care to perch; their food consists of seeds and grains they gather from the fields and their drink is a sip of water from some running brook. If I could not be a Scarecrow—or a Tin Woodman—my next choice would be to live as a bird does."

The gray dove had listened carefully to this speech and seemed to find comfort in it, for it hushed its moaning. And just then the Tin Woodman discovered Cayke's dishpan, which was on the ground quite near to him.

"Here is a rather pretty utensil," he said, taking it in his tin hands to examine it, "but I would not care to own it. Whoever fashioned it of gold and covered it with diamonds did not add to its usefulness, nor do I consider it as beautiful as the bright dishpans of tin one usually sees. No yellow color is ever so handsome as the silver sheen of tin," and he turned to look at his tin legs and body with approval.

"I cannot quite agree with you there," replied the Scarecrow. "My straw stuffing has a light yellow color, and it is not only pretty to look at but it crunkles most delightfully when I move."

"Let us admit that all colors are good in their proper places," said the Tin Woodman, who was too kind-hearted to quarrel; "but you must agree with me that a dishpan that is yellow is unnatural. What shall we do with this one, which we have just found?"

"Let us carry it back to the Emerald City," suggested the Scarecrow. "Some of our friends might like to have it for a foot-bath, and in using it that way its golden color and sparkling ornaments would not injure its usefulness."

So they went away and took the jeweled dishpan with them. And, after wandering through the country for a day or so longer, they learned the news that Ozma had been found. Therefore they straightaway returned to the Emerald City and presented the dishpan to Princess Ozma as a token of their joy that she had been restored to them.

Ozma promptly gave the diamond-studded gold dishpan to Cayke the Cookie Cook, who was so delighted at regaining her lost treasure that she danced up and down in glee and then threw her skinny arms around Ozma's neck and kissed her gratefully. Cayke's mission was now successfully accomplished, but she was having such a good time at the Emerald City that she seemed in no hurry to go back to the Country of the Yips.

It was several weeks after the dishpan had been restored to the Cookie Cook when one day, as Dorothy was seated in the royal gardens with Trot and Betsy beside her, a gray dove came flying down and alighted at the girl's feet.

"I am Ugu the Shoemaker," said the dove in a soft, mourning voice, "and I have come to ask you to forgive me for the great wrong I did in stealing Ozma and the magic that belonged to her and to others."

"Are you sorry, then?" asked Dorothy, looking hard at the bird.

"I am *very* sorry," declared Ugu. "I've been thinking over my misdeeds for a long time, for doves have little else to do but think, and I'm surprised that I was such a wicked man and had so little regard for the rights of others. I am now convinced that even had I succeeded in making myself ruler of all Oz I should not have been happy, for many days of quiet thought have shown me that only those things one acquires honestly are able to render one content."

"I guess that's so," said Trot.

"Anyhow," said Betsy, "the bad man seems truly sorry, and if he has now become a good and honest man we ought to forgive him."

"I fear I cannot become a good *man* again," said Ugu, "for the transformation I am under will always keep me in the form of a dove. But, with the kind forgiveness of my former enemies, I hope to become a very good dove, and highly respected."

"Wait here till I run for my Magic Belt," said Dorothy, "and I'll transform you back to your reg'lar shape in a jiffy."

"No—don't do that!" pleaded the dove, fluttering its wings in an excited way. "I only want your forgiveness; I don't want to be a man again. As Ugu the Shoemaker I was skinny and old and unlovely; as a dove I am quite pretty to look at. As a man I was ambitious and cruel, while as a dove I can be content with my lot and happy in my simple life. I have learned to love the free and independent life of a bird and I'd rather not change back."

"Just as you like, Ugu," said Dorothy, resuming her seat. "Perhaps you are right, for you're cert'nly a better dove than you were a man, and if you should ever backslide, an' feel wicked again, you couldn't do much harm as a gray dove."

"Then you forgive me for all the trouble I caused you?" he asked earnestly.

"Of course; anyone who's sorry just *has* to be forgiven."

"Thank you," said the gray dove, and flew away again.

**THE
END**

EL REY OOKS

Q.

What is the most enchanting fantasy trilogy in years?

Patricia McKillip's
The Quest of the Riddlemaster!